The Taming of Dominick

And Other Stories

The Taming of Dominick

Dominick

And Other Stories

FIRST EDITION

A Boner Book by
The Nazca Plains Corporation
Las Vegas, Nevada
2006

ISBN:1-887895-45-0

Published by:

The Nazca Plains Corporation ®
4640 Paradise Rd, Suite 141
Las Vegas NV 89109-8000

PUBLISHER'S NOTE
This is a work of fiction and fantasy. Names, characters, places, and incidents either are the products of the writer's imagination or are used fictitiously, and any resemblance to actual
persons, living or dead, business establishments, events or
locales is entirely coincidental. Always play safe.

Cover Art by Ross Johnston
Author Photograph by Don Ventura
Editor, Blake Stephens
Art Direction, Robert Steele

To Mr. John Embry-
for being there for me at the beginning of all of this...

Contents

Author's Foreword and Dedication

This story, "The Taming of Dominick", originally appeared and was serialized in "Manifest Reader" magazine, issues #37 and #38 back in the 1990's. I was totally honored to have my work appear in that magazine. At the time I felt it was my crowning achievement as my work was making its rounds in various magazines at the time. To see my work in print in "Manifest Reader" was truly flattering for an author of this particular genre. The story was actually written in an homage to a book entitled "That Day at The Quarry" written by Tom Shaw. Never before had a book affected me so deeply and so profoundly. After reading "That Day at the Quarry" four times (it mesmerized me that much) I decided that I wanted to write something equally as terrifying and something that would further ask the questions that "That Day at The Quarry" asked. "That Day at The Quarry" took place mostly outdoors where the unnamed (male) narrator is worked over in a sinister but erotic fashion by two of his buddies after he loses a game of poker. Three young guys agree to play a game of poker, the loser becoming the property of the two winners when the game is over, simple enough. The loser also has to allow the winners to work him over in any way they choose, to do anything they want to him, short of maiming him or murdering him of course. In my story, "The Taming of Dominick" the lead character is worked over indoors after he loses an old fashioned card game called "Go Fish" by his two buddies and he soon comes to realize how the most usual and everyday of household items can be turned into torture devices. "That Day at the Quarry" caused me to manifest a lot of questions in my mind where friendship between men was concerned and the fact that psychologically the majority of men out there are somehow attracted to pain. I believe, as do others that I have spoken to about this eccentric phenomenon that (supposedly) straight men can only show each other the kind of affection they crave in are-

1

nas where they are allowed to deliberately physically hurt one another and then affectionately hug, telling each other how well they did. As Gwyneth Paltrow said in the movie, "The Talented Mr. Ripley, "Why is it that when men play, they play at killing each other?" At the end of the story "That Day at The Quarry" the lead character who was worked over big-time remains friends with the two guys who hurt him so brutally and so humiliatingly. Is this possible I wondered. Could a guy lose at a game with the consequences that I have described, allow two of his good buddies to really work him over in the most horrid and degrading of ways and still remain friends with them? Because of those questions and others I knew that I had to write my own fantasy of this story. Dominick was a real person I knew years ago who became the model for this story. He was a young and handsome construction worker who had befriended me on the early morning train as we rode the rails together to our jobs. When I told Dominick that I was gay he was very cool on the subject, which was how my idea for him as the straight roommate in the following story was manifested. As time went on while I was friends with Dominick I re-read "That Day at the Quarry" for what would be my fourth time. Dominick was always curious about the books he saw me reading while we rode the train together. The cover picture on "That Day at the Quarry" showed a young handsome guy hanging upside down by his ankles, his arms bound and a gag tied over his mouth. Dominick of course noticed the cover of the book and with curiosity gleaming in his chestnut shaped brown eyes asked me what the book was about. I told him. I then asked him if he would participate in a card game like that with the consequences being so horrendous for the loser, if his buddies wanted to do something like that, would he do it. His gleaming smiling eyes suddenly turned to a look of terror and he said, "No." It was obvious to me that Dominick had buddies like the unnamed narrator in "That Day at the Quarry" had. His look of terror also fueled my desire to want to write my homage to "That Day at the Quarry." I lusted for Dominick during the time he was my train buddy up until he got married. I lusted for him so much that I made him the model for my story "The Taming of Dominick." I dedicate this story in particular to Mr. John Embry, then publisher of "Manifest Reader", for giving me the opportunity to have my work appear in such a truly erotic and over the top publication.

A Boner Book

The Taming of Dominick

It was six thirty AM. Wednesday morning. The shower had been turned off and that meant that my roommate Dominick was waiting for me in the bedroom. Every morning we go through the same kinky routine. We have been living together now for a little over a year. We met through a mixed up roommate service that accidentally paired a straight guy (Dominick) with a gay guy (me). Dominick is an extremely muscular construction worker with a somewhat hairy body and a thick sexy mustache. He's all of twenty-two years old and works for a company called "Green and Sons." When we first checked out the apartment and agreed to be roommates I told him that I was gay. I wanted that out of that way before we decided to take the place. Dominick said that my being gay didn't bother him in the least. He just wanted to make sure that I would pay my half of the rent every month. What I did in the sexual arena was my business. I agreed, telling him the same thing. On the nights when neither of us have dates we usually have dinner together. Dominick would always sit at the table bare chested, all sweaty and beat up looking after a hard day at work and I have to admit it drove me fucking wild. Other times he would parade around in just his white underpants with the kangaroo pouch in them, his big bulge paramount in them, before going to his room to go to sleep at night. He knew it was driving me wild because he would catch me looking at him. Neither of us said a word about it though. Until one of the nights neither of us had dates and we were sitting across from each other at the dinner table chowing down on take-out Chinese food. Dominick was sitting there bare chested as usual, wearing his worn looking, scruffy blue jeans and unlaced construction boots. He looked beat from a hard day's work of carrying cinder-blocks, swinging hammers, and just plain old sweating like crazy out in the hot sun.

"Man, this food really hits the spot Chris," he said to me after swallowing a mouthful of chicken fried rice and belching real loud. "The cold beer was a great idea too..."

I said that it was no problem as he took a gulp of his Budweiser.

"AHHHH, nice and fucking cold," he said and belched loudly again. "Fuck man, totally fuck, I'm hornier than a god-damned toad! Haven't seen that girl, what was her fucking name...since last week man..."

"Charlene," I said to him. "Her name is Charlene."

"Yeah, that's right, fuckin' tit lovin' Charlene..." Dominick said and ran the palm of one of his huge hands over his big brown pointy and very fleshy looking nipples.

"Tit lovin'?" I asked him with a smile.

"Yeah, fucking bitch loves to suck on my nips Chris," Dominick said with a sly looking smile and squeezed his nipples real tight between his thumbs and first two fingers of each hand, really squeezing the beef of them, getting the tips of them nice and accented. "Can you believe that shit? She loves to suck my nips till I can't take it...then she fuckin' sucks 'em some more. She bights on 'em too Chris. Oh fuck man, I got to admit though, it feels great and it gets me harder than steel in my goddamned under shorts!"

As he talked my cock was getting hard in my pants...
"See man, I thought that just guys loved tits you know," Dominick went on, sounding real brutish. "Fuck, Charlene is the first girl I ever met who loves to work a guy's nipples. After she works 'em and I'm harder than a diamond she makes me fuck her slow...real slow...and, sometimes as I'm fucking her the bitch tortures my nips with her fingernails. Heaven man, sheer fucking heaven..."

Dominick leaned back in his chair and squeezed his nipples real hard.

"Arrrrrhh yeah, wish she was here right now Chris," Dominick panted, sounding almost desperate. "I sure could use her mouth on these big fat nubs of mine right about now..."
Looking down at his nipples he twirled his big meaty fingers and thumbs on them.

"I know some guys who get off working other guy's nipples also," I said matter of factly.

"Oh yeah?" Dominick asked me. "Anyone I know Chris?"

"Well, me for one," I said and smiled slyly myself at him.

"Yeah, you'd like to work my big nipples eh Chris?" Dominick asked me. "I bet you'd love to chow down on 'em for a while...really lick at 'em too huh?"

"I wouldn't mind," I said to him. "And I wouldn't tell any-one..."

Dominick leaned forward with his elbows on the table, looking at me intensely.

"You know Chris, one time I even let that horny bitch

Charlene tie me up and work my nipples," Dominick said to me, knowing he was driving me wild. "That way when my nips were all sore and hurting I couldn't stop her from torturing the fuck out of 'em…"

I pushed my plate of food aside as Dominick slowly stood up and walked over to me, looking real menacing, his huge pecs bouncing almost involuntarily it seemed. I stood up as well, pushed my chair back away from the table, and Dominick sat down on the table where my plate had been. I was looking hungrily at his nipples, my mouth filling with saliva.
"Go ahead buddy, it's okay," Dominick whispered.

I placed my hands on his somewhat hairy chest. It felt like iron, his pecs felt magnificent as I caressed them a bit. I ran my hands over and under his huge male cleavage and Dominick placed his hands flat on the table as he tilted his head back. He closed his eyes and I squeezed his nipples with my thumbs and first two fingers of each hand, the same way he had been doing it to himself just seconds ago.

"Ohhhhh yeah, fuck yeah, feels great…" Dominick murmured and licked his lips real sexily. "I love to have my goddamned nips worked on."

"And I love workin' them for you Dominick," I said and leaned down.

I slurped one of Dominick's nipples into my mouth and swirled my tongue all over it as I squeezed his other one with my fingers and thumb. I poked my tongue against the tip of his nipple in my mouth and it was instantly hard, erect and somehow tasty. I sucked it like crazy, drooling over the nub and sucking up my saliva over and over and over.

"OHHHHHRRR fuck man, that feels enormous…you do

that better than Charlene...damn!!!" Dominick said breathlessly. "Don't forget the other one Chris..."

"I won't forget..." I said and quickly resumed sucking and slurping Dominick's nipple.

After I had sucked both his nipples to the point of being erotically sore Dominick yanked his long, fat, hard and thickly veined throbbing cock out of his jeans. He held the mammoth sized meat stick in his hand. It was oozing droplets upon droplets of pre cum like crazy, dripping all over the sides and shaft of it.

"Please man...please get me off..." Dominick pleaded.

"Oh God..." I whispered, looking at the giant piece of man-meat that Dominick had been blessed with between his muscular legs. "Oh fucking A man..."

I sat down in my chair, pulled myself forward, and leaned my head down over Dominick's throbbing meat stick. I licked the sides of it a few times, tasting his pre cum. It was delicious to say the least, kind of sweaty and sweet tasting at the same time. As I licked the hunky construction worker's shaft more droplets of his pre seed oozed like mad out of his piss hole. I knew he was close so I slurped that big pound of beef of his into my mouth and sucked it for all I was worth. I managed to deep throat him a few times without choking on the giant schlong. Needless to say the big lug was impressed with my prowess.

"OHHHHHHHRRR man, yeah," Dominick moaned in sheer ecstasy. "Everyday from now on man, every fucking god-damned day..."

Dominick's crank throbbed in my mouth with a life of it's own. As I sucked him and sucked him I reached up and squeezed one of his man-sized nipples...hard. At that moment he shot his load in gushes, filling and filling my mouth with it.

"OOOOOHHHHRRR YEAH YEAH!!!" Dominick groaned in a high pitched tone of voice. "OHHHHH man, yeah!!!"

It seemed to go on and on as he came and came, squirting ropes upon ropes of his thick creamy cum in my mouth. What I could not swallow oozed out of the sides of my mouth and dripped over my chin. Finally, when Dominick stopped shooting his giant load of ball juice his cock slipped slowly out of my mouth. We looked at each other, him up on the table in front of me and me sitting on the chair in front of him. Neither of us seemed to feel guilty or funny about what had just transpired between us.

"Everyday Chris, please man, do me like that everyday," Dominick pleaded, sounding demanding at the same time."Okay man, but there's something I want in return for sucking your nips and your giant meat everyday," I said to him.

"What is it man?" he asked me.

"Tits and cock aren't the only parts of a guy's body that I like," I said and lifted one of his booted feet in my hands.

I ran my hands over his unlaced scuffed up boot and into it, feeling his sweaty and moist white sweat sock. I took my fingers out of his boot and licked them, loving the funky taste of Dominick's foot sweat.

"Mmmm..." I crooned.

"Oh no Chris, don't fucking tell me you want to lick my damned smelly feet," Dominick said with that sly smile on his face. "Don't tell me you're one of those foot freaks I've heard so much about."

"Yeah, I like feet," I said, my hands moving over his foot that I was holding.

"Okay, I'll make you a deal now," Dominick said, sounding almost like a businessman. "Every morning after I shower you can work my nips for me and get me off like you just did. And, when I get home at night you can lick my rancid and stinky feet…"

I lifted his booted foot higher and kissed the top of it.

"Deal…" I said.

So, that's how Dominick and I started the routine that I mentioned earlier. Everyday it's the same thing and admittedly, I love it. I mean, how many gay guys out there get to lick a construction worker's nips, suck his cock and service his big feet for him?

I walked into Dominick's bedroom wearing just my briefs and found Dominick the same way, in his kangaroo pouch style white briefs. There's something real hot and erotic about a big muscle boy wearing nothing but a pair of sexy white briefs I got to say. His dark hair was still damp and matted to his head and beads of shower water glistened in his thick mustache. He was leaning on the dresser, his back to me. Fucking fuck man, his ass globes were exquisite looking in his briefs, like two honeydew melons.

"Good morning…"I said, placing a hand on his shoulder. Slowly, he turned around and we smiled at each other.

"Good fucking morning to you too," he said and I squeezed the beefy sides of each of his nipples. "MMMMMM…"

Dominick placed his big meaty hands on the dresser behind him, pushed his chest out, and closed his eyes in ecstasy as I squeezed his nipples a tad harder, getting to the tips of them by then.

"MMMMMM yeah, feels so fucking good..." he moaned softly.

I leaned down and slurped one of his nipples into my mouth while squeezing the other one with my fingers and thumb.

"OHHHHHRRR man, if my twisted buddies at the job-site knew about this they would probably freak," Dominick said and placed his huge hand on the back of my neck, gently squeezing it. "Imagine me, a straight shooter like me, letting another god-damned guy suck my big nips and cock...and at night having that same fucking guy lick my smelly feet clean for me..."

"Dominick..." I said softly and sucked the nub that was in my mouth real heartily.

"Yeah Chris?" he replied and squeezed the back of my neck again.

"Remember you told me how Charlene tied you up one time and really worked the fuck out of your nips?" I asked him and then sucked his nipple some more, making real slurpy sounds as I did it.

"Yeah, I remember," the studly guy said and ran his fingers through my hair. "Why man?"

"Do you think I could do that to you some time, tie you up and work your nipples till you can't take it?" I asked him.

I stopped sucking his nipple and looked at him hopefully. He seemed a bit taken aback by my new request but then he smiled real big and squeezed the back of my neck again, harder this time. I found that I liked it when he did that.

"Sure thing man, sure fucking thing…" Dominick said and roughly pushed my face back toward his attention demanding nipple.

I resumed sucking and licking his nipple.

"Yeah, I'll let you tie me up real good some time," my hunky roommate chuckled meanly.

When both of Dominick's nipples were erect, hard and pointy I slowly slid to my knees and pressed my face against the pouch of his briefs. The smell of fabric softener mixed with his body scent drove me into a frenzy. I licked the crotch of his briefs, running my hands over his muscular tree-trunk like legs. Dominick now squeezed his nipples as I slowly took his hard and throbbing meat out of the fly opening in his briefs.

"OHHHHHHH yeah, suck my big meat stick Chris…" Dominick moaned as I slurped his cock into my mouth, trailing my quivering lips gently over the crown part of it. "Get me off man, fucking get me off…"

Nothing like sucking some big construction worker's big meat first thing in the morning and getting him off…and every morning I do just that…get my hunky and handsome roommate off before he goes to work. And then in the evenings he brings me another real treat…

I'm always home from my office job before Dominick gets home and spend an hour or so waiting for him to come in. When he arrives home he's usually all sweaty looking from his hard day at the construction job-site. Most days he smells real ripe from working out in the heat all day. He goes to the kitchen first, gets an ice cold beer from the refrigerator, takes a few hearty gulps from it, burps real loud, and then settles down on the couch in the living room, his big booted feet propped up on the hassock I have put there just for this purpose.

"Man, what a day, what a real busy day," Dominick said and took another gulp of his beer. "I feel totally fucking wasted and beat to shit from the damned heat..."

He took off his shirt and tossed it on the floor as I knelt down at his feet. I ran my hands over his construction boots as he squeezed his nipples and ran the cold can of beer against them.

"Ahhhhh feels good, nice and cold..." Dominick said contentedly.

Slowly, I unlaced his boots and ran my hands over them again. Dominick watched in awe as I pressed my lips against the sides of his big boots a few times each, inhaling the scent of the warm leather.

"Man, I never knew anyone like you before in my life Chris..." Dominick said and sipped his beer. "That roommate service really did you a favor huh? You're definitely one of a fucking kind..."

I pulled his left boot off his foot and put it over my nose and mouth, inhaling his manly and funky foot odor. It smelled real musty and macho, like the man Dominick is. I licked the inside of his left boot as far in as my tongue could reach and then put it down on the floor. I proceeded to get his right boot off his other foot and sniffed and licked the inside of that one as well.

My cock was getting hard in my pants and I could see the huge bulge in Dominick's worn looking jeans as he watched me.

"Damn, those boots have been on my feet since early this morning," Dominick said and sipped his beer. "My feet sweat in those shit kickers all fucking live long day, hardy fucking har! They must stink like nobody's business and you're fucking licking and smelling them like they were air freshener…"

I smiled up at my handsome and muscular roommate and placed his right boot on the floor beside his left one. I then proceeded to press my nose against the bottom of Dominick's thick white sweat socked right foot, inhaling deeply the scent of sweat from his sock.

"Mmmmm…" I crooned and flicked my tongue over Dominick's smelly socked foot.

Dominick gulped down the rest of his beer, put the empty can on the floor beside the couch, and ran his hands over his nipples as I sniffed his socked feet.

"How do those socks of mine smell buddy?" Dominick asked me with a grin. "Do they really fucking stink or what?"

"Yeah, they sure do…" I said slowly. "But it's your scent and I love it…"

I sniffed Dominick's sweat socks all over, running my nose over his toes as I held his foot tight, the tops of his feet, and over and around his heels. I squeezed his socked feet and his socks felt warm and moist in my hands. Then, slowly I ran my hands under his pants legs and found the tops of his socks. I pulled them down slowly and slipped them off his big feet. The smell of Dominick's bare feet assaulted my nostrils yet I was drawn toward them like a magnet. The rancid scent of his sweaty feet

15

was just too much for me to take, yet I took it. I stuck out my tongue and ran it up and down and up and down the sides of Dominick's left foot first, flicking the tip of my tongue over the tops of his (cute) toes. Next, I sucked each of Dominick's toes like they were a cock, running my tongue over them while they were in my mouth.

"Ohhhhhh man, that feels so fucking good I gotta say," Dominick panted in ecstasy. "I cannot believe I let you do this shit to me…"

I slobbered over the big guy's feet and licked up my saliva like I was possessed; loving the taste of his feet sweat at the same time.

"Man oh man, the twisted guys at the job-site would never believe this…" Dominick murmured contentedly. "I am one lucky fucking guy that is for sure…"

When I was done cleaning Dominick's sweaty feet with my tongue I got us both a beer each and sat down next to him on the couch. We clapped our beer cans together and took a hearty gulp each.

"Same time tomorrow morning buddy?" Dominick asked me and squeezed one of his nipples, making the tip of it really bulge up.

"Same time buddy…" I replied and gave his nipples a squeeze each.

"Like those tits of mine eh buddy?" Dominick asked me, watching as I toyed with one of his nipples, twisting the tip of it real playfully.

"Yeah, I sure as shit do…" I replied.

Dominick smiled fiendishly and squeezed the back of my neck.

"Go on buddy, get back down there and lick my feet some more..." Dominick said sternly. "...feels so fucking good to have you doin' that while I scoff down my beer."

I put my beer down on the floor next to the couch, knelt in front of Dominick's bare feet, stuck out my tongue, and went back to work on his feet...giving them another good tongue bath.

"Ohhhhhh man, so fucking good..." Dominick droned. "Hey, pour some of your beer on my feet and lick that up too. Bet you'll love slurping your beer off my raunchy feet..."

And so, as I said, every morning I get to service my hunky roommate's nipples and every night I get to service his rancid and stinking feet. As time went on Dominick came to love being like a sadistic master to me, reveling in ordering me at his nipples and feet. When I mentioned again to him about letting me tie him up and work his nipples like his girlfriend Charlene once (or more than once I'm sure by now) did he somehow always managed to dodge the subject. I sort of got the feeling that it was okay by him to have me service his nipples, his cock and his feet, but he was not going to let me get him in such a comprising position as him being in bondage. I wanted Dominick to feel what it was like to be dominated. Actually I wanted him to feel dominated by me...the way I had come to feel so very dominated by him. It seemed it was never going to be though...until recently, when Dominick stupidly bit off more than he could chew and was dominated, not by me, but by two of his so called (twisted) buddies from his job. It was on a recent Saturday when he finally arrived home at one o'clock in the morning. Wearing a white tee shirt, worn blue jeans, and his tan colored construction boots Dominick came into the apartment and saw me sitting on the living room couch. I guessed that he thought I was waiting up for him. He walked slowly and (it seemed) painfully into the living room, a look of sheer agony mixed with utter exhaustion etched on his handsome face. He flopped down in the chair across from the couch and laid his feet on the hassock which was of course in front of the chair. Seeing the pain he was obviously in I looked at him with great concern.

"Dominick, what the hell happened to you?" I asked him, putting down the book I had been reading. "You look awful man…"

"Don't even ask Chris," Dominick said softly and put an arm over his eyes. "Shit…"

"You went out in the early afternoon for a game of cards with your two work buddies," I said, leaning forward on the couch. "Is that where you've been all this time?"

"Yeah, at Richie's house, with him and Bob," Dominick muttered. "FUCKERS…some buddies they turned out to be."
"What the hell happened?" I asked, getting up off the couch and going over to him.

I squatted down at his feet and began unlacing his boots.

"Oh man, Chris don't…" Dominick said slowly as I unlaced his boots, preparing to take them off his big feet. "It wasn't my fault…I agreed to all of it…fucking stupid of me…"

"What did you agree to?" I asked and slid his right boot off his foot.

When I saw that Dominick's foot was bare in the boot I

looked up at him quizzically. He took his arm away from his eyes and looked down at me as I looked at him.

"Dom, where are your socks?" I asked him, putting his boot down and beginning to unlace the other one.

"They kept 'em," Dominick replied. "My goddamned underpants too...as souvenirs...the fucking perverts..."

I slid his other boot off his foot and saw there was no sock on that foot either.

"I think you'd better explain all this to me man," I said, taking each of the guy's bare and smelly feet in my hands. "You look as if you're in intense pain..."

"I am man, I really am," Dominick said and I could see that he was actually choking back tears.

I could not believe this, my fucking rough and overly macho roommate sitting in front of me, practically crying. Then, I noticed something else.

"Dom, you have rope marks on your arms," I said, looking up at him as I gently squeezed his feet, taking in the sight of the rope burns along his huge biceps.

"Yeah, so I do," Dominick said and tried to smile. "At least Bob drove me home though, they didn't make me walk or take public transportation in this state..."

"Who?" I asked him.

"My two twisted so called buddies," Dominick seethed. "Fuckers worked me over Chris...like you would not fucking believe!!"

"Tell me," I said and kissed the tip of his big toe.

"Okay, as you know I had plans to spend Saturday afternoon with Richie and Bob at Richie's house for a game of cards and some lunch," Dominick began. "We had decided on a good old fashioned game called "Go Fish" like we played when we were kids. The object of that game is for one guy to lose all his cards, thus he winds up the loser."

I nodded as Dominick told his harrowing story...

Dominick had arrived at Richie's house at eleven thirty in the morning...good and early so they could start the game real quickly and then have lunch, and then kick back with a few cold beers of course. When Dominick got there Bob was already there. The three construction workers sat down at the kitchen table, the deck of cards in the center of the table. All three of the guys were glad to finally have a Saturday off and just to kick back and relax. With all the work and overtime they had been pulling in lately their well-toned bodies were aching and tired. Little did Dominick know as Richie dealt the cards just how very tired and achy he would be by the time the day was over. After they had all been dealt four cards each and the deck was placed in the center of the table they were ready to begin the game. They had decided that Richie would go first, Dominick would be second, and Bob third.

"Go ahead Richie, start the game," Bob said, looking intently at his cards.

"In a minute," Richie said, suddenly looking at Dominick and Bob very fiendishly. "I just came up with a really sick but great fucking idea...although you two will probably be chicken shit to go for it..."

"What kind of idea?" Dominick asked him. "And you know that I'm not chicken shit man!"

"Yeah, me too," Bob chimed in.

"Okay, lets make this game more intense," Richie suggested.

"You mean play for money?" Bob asked him.

"No, lets play the game, but the loser, the first guy to lose all his cards has to let the other two guys do whatever the fuck they want to him..." Richie said, looking at Dominick and Bob challengingly. "And I mean whatever the fuck they want to do, short of breaking his bones and murder of course... I read a story like that recently and I've wanted to try it out myself..."

"You have got to be joking," Bob said. "That sounds crazy."

"But interesting," Dominick said, looking at Richie intently, meeting his fiendish look. "I say lets do it..."

"Okay..." Bob chimed in. "But Richie, if you lose, are you prepared to take your punishment from me and Dominick?"

"Sure thing man, I ain't a damned wussy," Richie said. "I will take whatever the fuck the two of you can dish out. I just hope that if one of you loses you'll be able to take whatever the fuck I dish out. Because if one of you loses I'm calling the shots on the loser! Now, lets play cards boys."

"Okay, I'm in," Bob said and the fateful game began. When the game started Dominick already had two King cards so he figured he would definitely come out a winner...right!! They had agreed that the loser would have to allow the winners to do whatever they wanted to him except permanently damaging him or murdering him of course. They would be allowed to use anything in the house and the punishment would go on for as long as the winners decided that it would. Richie, dressed in white sneakers, blue jeans, and a black pull-over shirt, twenty-two years old with short blond hair and a muscular and hairless body looked worried when Dominick asked him if he had any fours. Richie handed Dominick two fours. Bob dressed in a short sleeved checkered shirt, black jeans, and black construction boots, twenty-three years old with black hair and a muscular and hairy body looked equally worried when Dominick made him hand over two of his ace cards. Yeah, Dominick was on the road to winning the game...or so he thought. Midway through the game things started to look grim for my handsome room-mate. He was down to only six cards and losing miserably. Richie and Bob looked at each other gleefully. It was as if they were hoping Dominick would wind up losing the game. It was at that moment that Dominick realized that his two (twisted) buddies had talked about all this before he had arrived for the card game. They had figured they would just take their chances and pray that my handsome roommate would come out the big loser. Dominick was breathing pretty heavily and nervously when he was down to two cards. Out of the corner of his eye he could see his two buddies snickering, knowing that it would be over at any moment now...and he would then have to let them do whatever the fuck they wanted to him. Dominick wondered what the two fuckers had planned. Judging from the looks on their faces he knew it would be nothing good. When Richie asked Dominick if he had any Queen cards Dominick handed him his Queen card, leaving the poor fuck with just one card, a Jack of clubs. Dominick looked at Bob with real terror in his eyes. Bob looked at Dominick smugly.

"Oh shit..." Dominick whispered.

"Tell me Dominick, do you have any Jack cards?" Bob

asked and he and Richie laughed hysterically, sounding totally sadistic.

Dominick handed Bob his Jack card, his last card, and sat slumped miserably in his chair. His two (twisted) buddies gave each other a high five and then looked at him fiendishly.
"Man, you really thought you were going to win this fucking thing," Richie said to Dominick mockingly.

"I was off to a good start," Dominick said, looking up at his so called buddy, his lips trembling as he spoke.

"But I'll bet you're not feeling all that slick now eh buddy?" Richie asked Dominick.

Dominick simply nodded and his two buddies stood up.

"I say lets do it…" Richie mimicked Dominick in a childish sounding type of voice.

"When do you want to start on him?" Bob asked Richie.

"Right now man, right fucking now," Richie replied, look- ing down at Dominick. "And we aren't going to stop till late…very fucking late…"

Dominick gulped hard, knowing that he had bitten off more than he would be able to chew.

"On your feet Dominick!!" Richie barked sternly. "From this moment on your sorry ass is ours. Is that clear?"

Dominick nodded as he stood up. Standing there, he watched as Richie opened a cabinet under the sink and took out a long pile of white cotton rope.

"Oh fuck..." Dominick whispered hoarsely. "You guys are goin' to tie me up???"

"Sure are buddy," Richie said happily. "As soon as you're stripped, down to your socks..."

"You've got to be fucking kidding me!!" Dominick said in utter disbelief.

His two buddies looked at each other and smiled. Then they looked back over at their prey.

"Strip Dominick," Richie ordered. "NOW!!!"

"Come on you guys, fun's fun and all that but..." Dominick began and suddenly Richie was standing nose to nose with him.

"You fucking pussy man!!" Richie snarled at Dominick. "You fucking agreed to the rules of the game. You're the guy who said it sounded interesting and that we should do it!"

"I didn't think that I would have to strip balls ass naked and get tied the fuck up!!" Dominick snapped back at his so called buddy.

"I told you that you could leave your socks on man, you won't be totally naked, ha!! But that's just the beginning of what you're in for buddy," Richie said angrily and with total authority in his voice. "Now make like a Chippendales dancer and strip!" With that, Richie reached up, quickly grabbed one side of Dominick's thick mustache and gave it a hard yank, meanly pulling out a few strands of thin hairs.

"AAAAAAAYYRRRRRR!!!!" Dominick roared and hobbled a few steps backward, his hand over his mustache, looking at

Richie in disbelief.

"You are going to find that we really mean business buddy," Richie said, standing next to Bob.

With his hands trembling Dominick shucked off his tee shirt, revealing his slightly hairy and very muscular chest, his two pointy brown nipples, his huge pecs, and flat stomach. He leaned down, unlaced his boots, and pulled them off his big feet. As his two buddies watched he unbuttoned his jeans, pushed them down to his ankles and stepped out of them. Looking at his two buddies blankly he grabbed the sides of his pouch style white briefs and pushed them down to his ankles. He stepped out of them and then stood before Richie and Bob wearing just his white sweat socks which had wound up pushed down close to his ankles when he had stripped off his jeans. He didn't feel the need to pull his socks up. His cock was semi hard with fear between his legs and his two big juicy balls were hanging down low. Dominick angrily kicked his clothes away from himself and looked at his two buddies, wondering what was about to happen.

"Arms crossed and up behind your back buddy boy..." Richie said as he and Bob approached Dominick, Richie holding the rope menacingly.

Dominick did as he was told and his two buddies stood at his sides, prepared to begin. Richie handed Bob some rope and they had a grand old time roping Dominick's arms up behind him.

"Man oh man, did you see the fucking look of despair on his face when he realized he'd lost the game?" Richie asked Bob. "Fucking guy really thought he was going to win."

"Yeah, I know..." Bob said his face right near the side of

Dominick's face, close enough to kiss his cheek if he wanted to. "Say Dom, what did you have planned for me and Richie if one of us had lost the game?"

"Never mind that..." Richie said before Dominick could reply. "This poor fucking guy should be totally concerned with what we're going to do to him...it ain't going to be fun for him that he can be assured of. But it sure as fuck is going to be fun for you and me."

When they were done tying him Dominick's arms were crossed uncomfortably up behind his back, tied tightly in three places. They had also tied ropes over Dominick's shoulders and under his bushy armpits and ran the slack of it down to his bound up arms. They had tied the slack around his huge muscular arms to keep them way up where they wanted them. There was rope also tied under Dominick's big male cleavage and around and around his biceps, making his nipples really stick out for what they had in mind for them. As they tied Dominick his cock grew hard, fat, and it throbbed, mostly in fear I would think. A lot of guys, when they're really scared tend to a lay a hard-on for some reason. His balls were now hanging low and fearfully down under his hard cock. Dominick watched as his two buddies squatted at his sides, tied rope around the top of his ball sac, around his waist, and tied it off behind his back, pulling it real tight, trapping his poor balls just under his ass crack so they were sticking out behind him, nice and inviting like.

"Shit, he really looks good and fucking helpless," Bob said as he and Richie straightened up at Dominick's sides.

"Sure does doesn't he?" Richie asked agreeably. "And scared too. He looks really fucking scared. Bet you're wondering just what the fuck we have planned for you eh buddy boy?"

"Yeah, the thought had crossed my mind," Dominick said

meekly, trying not to sound too scared. "Seeing as you've got me all stripped and sexy and tied up and all…"

His two buddies snickered at his sides and then Dominick was shocked as they leaned down and each of them meanly slurped one of his fat pointy nipples into their mouths. They sucked, nipped, and bit down hard and ferociously with their front teeth on his nipples.

"OOOOHHHHHRRRR SHIT…" Dominick groaned and tottered on his socked feet. "OHHHH GOD…"

The two men ran their hands over Dominick's bulging and bound biceps, slapping them and squeezing them hard and painfully as they sucked the fuck out of his nipples.

"Fuck guys, I didn't know you two had gone faggot," Dominick muttered, watching as they worked his nipples harder and harder and chills coursed through his muscular being.

"Who said we went faggot?" Richie asked, the nipple he'd been working on now held tightly and painfully between his thumb and first finger. "This is just the beginning of the torture the loser, you, has to endure…and having your tits sucked like a woman's must feel real humiliating huh? And may I say buddy boy that these big tits of yours are just as tasty and nubile as my girlfriends?"

With that Richie laughed and eagerly slurped Dominick's nipple back into his mouth.

"I wonder what all our girlfriends would think if they could see this shit…me all tied up and my two good buddies chowing down on my damned tits…AAAAARHHHH FUCK…"
Dominick gasped and leaned his head back.

About ten tit sucking minutes later they were still working Dominick's nipples with their mouths. By then his nipples were feeling pretty sore, numb and erect and over-worked actually. He knew better than to ask his buddies to stop. They were now standing in front of him, leaning down, his nipples still in their mouths. They were clamping my roommate's nipples between their front teeth and pulling meanly on them...forcing Dominick to take a few steps forward. This was definitely not the stuff of what he was used to where me or his girlfriend working his nipples was concerned.

"AAAAARRRRHHH SHIT!!!" Dominick roared. "Easy you guys, easy with my damned nips..."

Dominick was forced to walk another few steps on his toes, feeling as if his two buddies were going to rip his poor nipples right off his chest with their teeth.

"AAAARRRGGGHHHH!!!" he bellowed loudly.

When they stopped another fifteen minutes later Dominick's nipples were swollen, numb and more erect than he had ever seen them before. His two buddies laughed gleefully, squeezed the aching tips of his nipples, and congratulated each other on a job well done. They had accomplished just what they had wanted with poor Dominick's nipples.

"Lookin' good..." Richie commented, squeezing one of Dominick's nipples hard, making him gasp pretty loud in pain. "Now for the next part of this shit. Bob, do your thing while I get them."

Bob squatted down in front of Dominick, gobbled his big cock into his mouth, and began sucking it as Richie walked over to the cabinet where he had gotten the rope from earlier.

"Ohhhhhh shit, ohhhhh fuck..." Dominick grunted loudly as Bob chowed down on his big meat. "You two fuck-heads are really shocking the shit out of me today...look at you fuckin' suckin' my big ol' meat, nursing on my damned cock!"

Dominick reeled in ecstasy (and lets face it, confusion) as Bob sucked him like a pro, not bothering to turn around and see what Richie was taking out of the cabinet. He was really enjoying the feeling as Bob sucked his cock, causing his bound balls to crash against his ass crack as he did so. But then, Richie came and stood beside Dominick, one hand held behind his back.

"Liking that eh buddy boy?" Richie asked Dominick as Bob chowed and chowed heartily on his huge cock. "Bet your girlfriend never sucked you so damned good..."

"Oh yeah," Dominick replied breathlessly, looking down at Bob working on his cock, feasting on it. "Fucking A!!"

"Then you're going to hate this," Richie said and showed Dominick the two clip-on clothespins he had been holding behind his back.

"Ohhhhh shit, no man..." Dominick moaned in fear as Richie opened the clothespins and held them directly over and around the meat of his swollen and erect nipples. "Please Richie, no..."

Ignoring Dominick's whimpering he closed the clothespins on the tender flesh of the poor guy's nipples and let go of them.

"AAAAYYYYYRRRRR!!!" Dominick screamed loudly in a man's pain. "OHHHRRRR you fuckers..."

Richie clapped Dominick hard on one of his pecs, getting them jiggling a bit, squatted down next to Bob, and the two men took turns sucking Dominick's big meat stick, alternating it in and out of their mouths. Dominick was in pain and ecstasy at the same time. As he stood there tottering on his socked feet he helplessly shot his load.

"OHHHHHRRRRR SHIT, I'm creaming you guys, I'm fucking creaming like a son of a bitch here!!" Dominick ranted as Richie held his cock tightly in his fist, making him cum on the kitchen floor. "OHHHHHHHRRRR SHHHIIITTTT!!!!"

Dominick reeled in ecstasy, his head flung back, his muscular body bucking real sexily back and forth, the clothespins on his nipples swinging wildly, making his nipples ache more and more. Richie held and squeezed Dominick's cock tighter and tighter, forcing every possible drop of cream out of it.

"Ooooohhhh fuckers," Dominick gasped when Richie finally let go of his cock.

His cock was tingling and his nipples were alive and beyond tingling in the confines of the clothespins. His balls were now aching miserably under his ass crack and he would have done anything at that moment to have them untied. Richie and Bob stood up at Dominick's sides and Richie ordered Dominick to get down on his knees and clean the cum up off the floor. Dominick looked at his buddy angrily.

"If you didn't want my damned cream all over your floor what the fuck did you get me off for?" Dominick asked and Richie slapped one of his pecs good and fucking hard. "OHHHRRRRRR…"

Dominick slowly slid to his knees, leaned forward, and began licking up his cum from the linoleum.

"Shit man, look at those hairy ass globes of his Bob,

just asking for some attention," Richie said to Bob, noting how Dominick's butt cheeks were up in the air, his tied balls just under them looking real sexy and helpless.

"Yeah, let's give them some painful attention..." Bob said eagerly.

As Dominick leaned over on his knees licking and slurping his mess of cum off the floor the clothespins on his nipples were dangling just above the floor, pulling down painfully on his poor tortured nipples. Suddenly, Richie whacked him hard across the ass cheeks with his leather belt, followed quickly by Bob.

"YOWWWWWWW!!!" Dominick screeched and sat up on his haunches.

He saw that they had both removed their belts from the loops of their jeans and were holding them in their hands, folded over.

"Get back down there and finish cleaning my floor asshole!!" Richie yelled and rapped Dominick hard across his bound muscular arms with his belt.

"UUUUHHRRRRRRRR!!!" Dominick ranted through clenched teeth and reluctantly did as he was told.

Richie and Bob beat Dominick's hairy ass cheeks savagely and wildly with their belts as he tried his best to finish licking up all his cum. He screamed in pain between licks and laps as his two buddies beat his ass harder and harder with each blow administered from their belts. Dominick's lips started trembling, making it difficult to finish the job at hand. When one of their belts connected slightly with his exposed bound balls he cried out sounding almost pitiful, only to receive more hard whacks across his already very wounded ass cheeks. When all his cum was off the floor they stopped whacking his ass cheeks and Dominick slowly sat up on his knees. He was shaking and trembling, big tears flowing out of his chestnut shaped dark eyes.

"I wouldn't even make my faggot roommate eat his or my cum," Dominick muttered under his breath. "What a fucking horrible way to eat..."

"On your feet buddy boy," Richie said. "We're just getting started on you. By the time we send you home to that roommate of yours you're going to be exhausted and hurting like never before in your life."

Dominick got to his feet and stood docilely between his two best (twisted) buddies. Richie took the clothespins off Dominick's nipples and tossed them on the table. Dominick's nipples were now more than swollen and overly erect. They were swollen to twice their normal size and searing hot pain was coursing through them after just having had the clothespins taken off them. Richie and Bob tweaked the tips of them hard, toyed with them with their fingers, and then meanly slurped them into their mouths again.

"AAAAAARRRHHHHHH ohhhhhhhh shit..." Dominick roared as they tortured his nipples all over again with their mouths, teeth and tongues.

My roommate stood there in agony, tottering on his socked feet, dizziness setting in as they worked his poor nipples more and more, harder and harder.

"AAAARRRHHHHHH!!! Why'd I have to go and agree to this shit??" Dominick ranted wildly.

When they stopped working his nipples (fifteen minutes later) they looked at them and squeezed them hard.

"Shit, his tits won't be the same for days Richie," Bob commented.

"Weeks..." Richie said, and quickly grabbed the clothespins off the table.

"Ohhhhhh no. no..." Dominick whimpered and Richie clipped the clothespins back onto his aching nipples. "AAAAYYYYRRRRR!!!"

"Come on Bob, I just had another great fucking idea," Richie said, moving Dominick over to a kitchen drawer by his arm, followed by Bob. "There are so many things in an average household that you can use to torture a guy with."

With that, Richie opened the kitchen drawer and took out two big serving spoons. He handed one to Bob.

"What the fuck are you going to do with those things? Dominick asked Richie.

In response Richie rubbed the smooth bottom of the spoon he was holding against one of Dominick's big pecs. "Ohhhhhh shit..." Dominick moaned and Richie slapped his pec hard with the spoon. "OHHHRRRRRRR!!!!"

"Come on Bob, do his other one," Richie egged Bob on. "Look at how it makes the clothespins on his tits jiggle..."
Bob raised his plastic spoon and brought it down hard on Dominick's other pec. Dominick screamed and reeled in pain as the two men really started beating on his pecs hard, really whaling into them with brute force. He stood propped against a kitchen counter as his two buddies beat the bottoms, tops, and sides of his pecs, all around his big male cleavage to be exact. Sweat was starting to roll off Dominick as he panted heavily,

wanting the torture to end at that moment. Looking down he saw how red his pecs were becoming as they beat them harder and harder with each blow. This time he screamed pitifully and in agony when the blows started stinging, practically burning because of the redness already all over his pecs.

"G-guys please..." Dominick panted as they continued beating the shit out of his pecs.

When they stopped a while later Dominick's pecs were crimson red, the redness sure to turn into bruises by the next day. He stood there panting, trembling, and even crying. He felt totally stupid for having allowed himself to get into this mess. The two men put down the serving spoons, took Dominick by his arms, slumped him over the table where they had just played the game of cards that had gotten my roommate into this predicament, and roped his dangling feet together at the ankles. Dominick clenched his teeth and screamed through them as his two buddies picked up their leather belts and began beating the backs of his thighs.

"RRRRRRHHHHHH!!!!" he screamed loudly, squirming on the table like a fish out of water.

"Man, he's going to be a fucking mess by the time all this is over," Bob laughed and rapped the back of Dominick's thighs hard with his belt.

By the time they stopped the backs of Dominick's thighs were as red as his ass cheeks and his pecs. The two men held him between themselves by his upper arms as he gasped for breath, felt dizzy, and sweated profusely. He managed to balance himself on his bound feet as the two men ran their hands over his wounded chest.

"Th-this is too much..." Dominick croaked miserably as

Richie took the clothespins off his nipples again and searing hot pain coursed through them. "AAAAYYYYYRRR!!!"

When the pain diminished a bit Dominick meekly said, "Thank you" to Richie for having taken the clothespins off his nipples. Richie held Dominick balanced his arms around my roommate as Bob squatted in front of him and gave his cock a few hearty sucks. Dominick was hard as a diamond again in seconds. His balls ached miserably though, still tied and trapped under his ass crack.

"Okay Bob, on your feet," Richie said. "I don't want our good buddy here to shoot another load so soon."

Bob got to his feet and stood beside Richie who was still holding Dominick balanced on his bound feet.

"You ready to have some more fun with him?" Richie asked Bob.

"Am I?" Bob asked anxiously. "Man, you don't have to ask me twice…just seeing him like this, all trussed the fucked up like a roped steer is driving me nuts…"

Richie smiled and patted Bob on the back.

"Man, I knew that I could count on your for this," Richie said to Bob. "I'm just glad it wasn't you who lost the card game."

"Me too man, me too…" Bob replied, a look of relief on his face.

Dominick looked angrily at his two so called buddies as they stood there openly mocking him, talking about him as if he were not there.

"Come on and help me get him slumped over the table again," Richie said to Bob as he grabbed Dominick by one arm with both hands. "Only this time we have to spread his legs apart..."

Bob grabbed Dominick's other arm with both hands and the two men hoisted him off the floor.

"UHHHHHHH..." Dominick grunted as his tied feet left the floor.

"God, this slab of meat really weighs," Richie chortled as they lugged their buddy back over to the table.

Moments later Dominick was slumped half on and half off the table, his legs dangling off the end of it and spread wide as far as possible. His socked feet were each tied to one of the table legs, keeping his legs spread out. His upper body was still all roped up and he was beginning to feel numbness in his arms and shoulders. His bound and aching balls were highly visible under his exposed ass crack and exposed asshole. Dominick wondered what the fuck he was in for now as Richie rummaged through a kitchen drawer with Bob at his side. He squirmed miserably on the table and then gulped in total fear when he saw what Richie took out of the drawer. Richie held up a pair of metal (rounded at the end) salad tongs. He clicked them together a few times to demonstrate to Bob what they were going to do...to poor Dominick's balls.

"When you've got one of his nuts between these things pull down or to the sides on it but be careful," Richie said. "We want it to hurt him but not to damage the poor guy for life... Dominick may want to be a father at some point..."

The two guys laughed as they approached the table.

Dominick looked at them in outright horror as they stepped behind him.

"You ready for some sick fun buddy boy?" Richie asked Dominick, holding up the salad tongs.

Dominick simply looked at him angrily and then faced forward, a feeling of dread swimming through him. Richie handed the tongs to Bob and told him he could go first torturing Dominick's nuts. Seconds passed and then Bob was squatting behind Dominick.

"God almighty, he looks fucking great all roped up and helpless Richie," Bob said breathlessly. "What the fuck is up with that?"

"It's the feeling of power you have over a guy like him man," Richie explained. "The feeling of awesome power…" Dominick felt the cold metal of the tongs close around one of his nuts and squeeze it hard.

"OHHHHHRRRRRRR!!!" Dominick roared in agony. Bob used the tongs to pull Dominick's nut down as far as possible. Then, he moved it slowly from side to side, torturing the guy unspeakably.

"OHHHHHRRRRRR GOD, you bastards," Dominick croaked in a high pitched tone of voice.

Sweat poured off Dominick's forehead and into his eyes, he cried like a baby, and squirmed miserably on the table. While his nut was enclosed in the tongs Richie told Bob to hold it steady and began tonguing it hard, applying awful pressure to it, getting more squeals of pain out of my roommate. Dominick could actually feel his testicle swelling up from the awful tortures it was enduring. Finally, Bob released his nut and handed the tongs to Richie. Richie quickly began torturing Dominick's other nut while Bob licked it painfully. Dominick laid his head against the table top and shook and cried... Richie released his nut after a while and then handed the tongs back to Bob. The guy immediately encased Dominick's first nut between the tongs again. Dominick screamed in a rage of pain again... While Bob tortured Dominick's nut Richie stood up and looked down at him squirming atop the table. Dominick craned his head back and saw him look at his exposed asshole and Richie's eyes lit up gleefully. Dominick knew that the bastard had just thought of another means of torturing him... Not to mention the outright embarrassment and utter humiliation of having his buddy looking at his on display and gaping asshole. Bob tortured Dominick's nuts alternately for a good twenty minutes or so and then when they were swollen beyond reason he told Richie he thought he ought to stop. Richie took one look at Dominick's poor balls, laughed loudly, and agreed with Bob.

"I have another idea though before we take him out of the kitchen," Richie said, pointing at Dominick's gaping asshole.

"Oh man, you are a fiend," Bob said with a wicked grin on his face. "I am really fucking glad that I didn't lose that card game..."

Moments passed and then Richie had collected all he would need. He and Bob greased up their fingers with some Mazola oil and proceeded to prod Dominick's stink hole open and wide for their sadistic plan.

"OHHHHHHH..." Dominick groaned as Richie plunged his middle finger deep into his most private crevice, prodding it like crazy, driving him batty.

Dominick's cock was hard as a rock under him and pointing straight down at the floor...a large bucket under it. When

Richie picked up the big yellow funnel he told Bob that my room-mate's hole was ready. As Richie inserted the stem end of the funnel deep into Dominick's hole Dominick himself looked with anguish at the six pack of beer on the table in front of him.

"We are going to get you good and fucking pissed buddy boy," Bob said and picked up the first can of beer. "Real pissed..."

"OHHHHHH no, no, no..." Dominick sighed weakly, his head still lying on the table.

Bob opened the can and stepped next to Richie.

"Okay, the funnel will hold in there, his ass cheeks are tight enough I think, ha!" Richie said. "Give him a good hearty drink. Get ready buddy boy, this beer is super cold..."

Bob slowly poured the contents of the can into the funnel and into Dominick's hole.

"AAAARRRGHHHHH!!!!" Dominick ranted and his head sprang up off the table. "Fuckers are filling my bladder up with beer!!"

In moments the first can of beer was empty and Richie quickly opened the second one. He poured it through the funnel also.

"AAAARRHHHHHH!!!!" Dominick roared as his head spun.

After the third can of beer had been poured Dominick had to piss like crazy and he was feeling sort of drunk. Inside himself he felt his stomach churning like mad. As Richie poured a fourth can of beer into the funnel Dominick pissed long, hard and frothy into the bucket under the table.

"AAAHHHHHH!!!" Dominick gasped as he was filled and he pissed at the same time.

It seemed like the pissing would go on forever as Dominick urinated uncontrollably into the large bucket.

"OOOOHHHHRRR you fuckers," Dominick whimpered as he watched Richie walk over to the refrigerator. "Wh-what now? What the fuck now?"

In reply to his question Richie filled a large glass with ice water, put a straw in the glass, and set it in front of Dominick's trembling lips.

"Drink up buddy boy," Richie said as Bob was pouring the final can of beer into the funnel.

"God," Dominick muttered and closed his lips around the straw.

As he drank the ice water he pissed again into the bucket. Finally, all the beer was gone and so was the ice water. Dominick breathed heavily and sweated like mad as he pissed again and again into the bucket. The sound of his piss filling the bucket was sexy and kinky somehow. His two buddies laughed hysterically. After a while more of pissing Richie slid the funnel out of Dominick's asshole and pulled his ass cheeks even further apart.

"AAAARRRRHHHH..." Dominick gasped angrily as his poor hole was opened wider.

"Man, its sopping wet in there with beer," Richie commented. "You know Bob; we can't let this moist pussy like hole of his go to waste…"

"Fucker, that's a crappy way to talk about my asshole!" Dominick piped up, sounding totally irate.

"What do you have in mind now you fiendish bastard?" Bob asked Richie with a shit eating grin on his face.

"Open the refrigerator and look in the fruit and vegetable bin," Richie replied, holding Dominick's ass cheeks painfully spread apart. "See what I have in there, if you get my drift…"

"You bastard," Dominick gasped, turning his head and looking at Richie angrily. "You wouldn't…that's my goddamned shit chute you're talking about here…"

"And get some ice cubes out of the freezer while you're at it…" Richie said to Bob.

Dominick pursed his lips together in anguish and Bob opened the refrigerator. While Bob was rummaging in the refrigerator Richie leaned over Dominick's exposed asshole and plunged his tongue into it.

"OHHHHHHHH…" Dominick groaned as Richie stole a few licks and slurps from his beer wet hole. "Fucker, think you're eating a goddamned pussy? Think again!!!"

Dominick pissed again into the bucket as Richie slurped the fuck out of his hole.

"Mmm…tastes as nasty as my girlfriend's pussy," Richie said mockingly.

Bob came over to the table with a fat cucumber, a long carrot, and a few ice cubes.

"We'll start with these…" Richie said, taking one of the ice cubes from Bob.

He inserted the ice cube into Dominick's hole quickly followed by a second one. As the ice cubes disappeared into his hole Dominick felt a chill shoot up his spine and he cringed on the table. He curled his sock covered toes back as a third ice cube was inserted into his hole.

"Okay Bob, you can have the honor of devirginizing our boy's hole with that cucumber," Richie said, grabbing Dominick's ass cheeks again and yanking them wide and far apart.

Dominick's mangy rosebud of an asshole seemed to be yawing at the two men…

"OHHHHHRRRRR no, no, no!!!" Dominick roared and pleaded as Bob began inserting the cucumber into his hole. "AAAAARRRHHHH shit you guys, my poor asshole!!"

Dominick pissed again and again into the bucket as Bob pushed the cucumber slowly into his asshole. Dominick felt beyond dizzy at that moment and he thought for sure that he was going to pass out from the intense pain. But then Richie scurried under the table, gobbled Dominick's piss saturated cock into his mouth and began sucking it as Bob turned the cucumber around and around in his stretched hole, fucking the poor guy beyond reason with it.

"AAARRHHHHGGGHHHH…" Dominick gushed, drooling at the mouth as he was fucked and sucked like mad.

He shot a second load, as big as the first one, right into the bucket under his cock while Richie held his aching cock in hand. Right after he was done shooting his load he pissed profusely again into the bucket. Bob had the cucumber a little more than halfway into Dominick's hole at that point. Dominick was sweating, dizzy, and practically in a stupor of sorts at that point. When Bob pulled the cucumber out of his hole Richie inserted the carrot. It tickled Dominick going in but the rough edges on the damned thing drove him nuts when Richie began thrusting his hole with it. When Dominick had agreed to all of this he had no idea of what he would be in for if he had lost the card game. He knew at that moment though that it would be a long time before he agreed to another game of cards with those two supposedly straight buddies of his… Dominick definitely got the feeling that he was in the clutches of two sadistic faggots. When Richie finally pulled the carrot out of Dominick's hole it was more than ten minutes later. Dominick's hole had been drenched, fucked, eaten, and rubbed raw with a carrot. It felt awful in there and he knew that when the time came that he would have to take a dump that it would be pretty painful for a few days. Richie and Bob threw the cucumber, the carrot and the empty beer cans in the trash and then squatted behind Dominick to lick and torture his balls for a while before untying him from the table…

"Ohhhhhhhhrrrrr shit," Dominick groaned as his swollen balls were tongued horribly. "Faggots…"

A few minutes later Dominick was off the table and standing between his two buddies. They held him steady by his arms, rubbing his big chest.

"You okay so far Dominick?" Bob asked him, sounding somewhat concerned.

Dominick nodded weakly.

"You look thirsty Dominick," Richie said mockingly. "Do you want something to drink before we get to the next round of what you're in for?"

"Y-yeah, that sounds good, maybe some cold water or..." Dominick began but stopped in mid sentence when he saw that Richie was looking at the bucket he had pissed so profusely into.

"Oh man Richie, you're goin' to make the guy drink his own piss?" Bob asked.

"I-I won't..." Dominick sputtered. "Please Richie..."

Richie viciously grabbed a handful of Dominick's sweat soaked hair, pulled it upward and yanked the poor guy's head back...hard.

"AAARRRRHHHHH..." Dominick ranted through clenched teeth.

"Get the fuck down there and start gulping down that mess you goddamned card game loser!" Richie said directly into Dominick's ear. "You are going to do it and everything else that we tell you to do...buddy boy..."

Richie let go of Dominick's hair and my roommate slowly knelt down over the bucket. When he lowered his head to begin drinking his piss out of the bucket Richie pushed the back of his head down hard, really getting Dominick's face into the piss. Dominick made huffing and glubbing sounds as Richie held his face in the piss. After a few seconds Richie pulled Dominick's head up. His handsome face and his mustache were soaked with and stinking of his piss.

"Say buddy boy, how does that slop of yours taste huh?" Richie asked in a mocking tone and before Dominick could say a word he pushed the guy's face back down into the bucket. "Come on you loser, I want to hear some real slurping sounds out of you," Richie said sternly. "Chug down that fucking mess. It is your piss and cum in that bucket after all."

When Richie was satisfied that Dominick had chugged down enough of the piss he hauled him up to his feet and looked at Bob. Dominick's face and mustache were soaked and stinking of piss. A few beads of his cum were stuck in his mustache and he was breathing heavily, choking back more tears, tears of humiliation one would think.

"Come on, let's take him upstairs to the bathroom and work on him there next," Richie said to Bob.

"Ohhhh please," Dominick begged as the two men grabbed him by an arm and a leg each.

They carried Dominick between themselves out of the kitchen, through the living room, and up the stairs toward the bathroom. Dominick's face and mustache were soaked and stinking of the rancid piss and the inside of his mouth tasted like a nightmare.

"Strong fuckers you two are..." Dominick groaned as they carried him up the stairs. "You fuckers...made me drink my piss..."

In the bathroom they put Dominick down on the tile floor. He was able to feel how cold the floor was even through his thick white sweat socks.

"Okay Bob, there's plenty of stuff in here that we can use on him," Richie said. "You ready?"

"Sure am," Bob said.

"I-I have to piss..." Dominick croaked and stepped in front

of the open toilet.

He pissed a long white stream into the bowl as Richie picked up the plastic bottle of liquid soap from the vanity.

"Man, I'll just bet that that cock of yours is all messy and dirty from all that pissing you've been doing..." Richie said, and as Dominick turned around he grabbed the guy's semi hard cock in his hand and squeezed it tight.

"AAAARRHHHHH!!!" Dominick roared as Richie squeezed his cock harder, getting a few beads of piss to form on the tip of it.

Bob watched intently as Richie shook the beads of piss off Dominick's cock, handling it not all that gently at that, and then held the liquid soap dispenser directly over his open and gaping piss slit.

"OHHHRRRRRR NO NO!!" Dominick yelled insanely at the two men.

Richie squeezed Dominick's cock and then pushed down on the liquid soap dispenser. As he squeezed Dominick's cock his piss slit opened and closed, literally eating the liquid soap that Richie was pouring into it.

"OHHHHRRRRRR you bastard!!!" Dominick spat at Richie. "Th-this is sick man!!"

"Oh shit, your cock is going to be burning like crazy every fucking time you piss buddy boy..." Bob laughed and gave one of Dominick's sore nipples a hard squeeze.

"Oh shit is right you fucker, I have to piss like crazy already," Dominick announced and Richie quickly let go of his cock and put the soap dispenser down on the vanity.

Holding Dominick's upper arms Richie positioned him in front of the open toilet. Dominick clenched his teeth and pissed.

"AYYYYYRRRR!!!" he screamed, his voice bouncing off the tile walls.

As he pissed it felt like the inside of his cock was on fire. "AAAAYYYYYY shit..." Dominick croaked as he pissed more and more.

When he was done pissing again Richie waited for Dominick's cock to get soft. He then positioned Dominick in front of the vanity and laid his flaccid cock on top of the edge of it. Dominick looked at him questioningly.

"Just hold still buddy boy," Richie said, looking at Dominick and stroking his sweat soaked hair in the back. "Hold real fuck-ing still."

Then, Richie brought his palm smashing down on Dominick's cock.

"AAAAYYYYYYRRRR!!!" Dominick screamed in a high pitched tone of voice.

When Bob whapped Dominick's cock with the palm of his hand Dominick hopped around in pain, trying to keep his poor tortured cock on top of the edge of the vanity. Richie gave his cock another good open palmed whap and then so did Bob. When they saw that Dominick's cock was looking slightly purple at the tip after a few more hard whaps they stopped. Dominick was crying profusely, snot was dripping out of his nose and he was sweating like crazy by then.

"Good God almighty..." Dominick squealed with his head hanging down. "Some fucking good buddies you two are!!"

To substitute torturing his cock they took turns whacking his ass cheeks, his thighs, and upper arms with a big old back brush that Richie had hanging in the shower. Dominick stood with his bruised and burning cock lying on the vanity top as his two buddies whacked him over and over with the hard bristles of the back brush. They again had him hopping around in pain, grunting and gasping, and screaming in agony. Bob found a tube of heat rub in the medicine cabinet and Richie went on pummeling Dominick with the back of the brush.

"Hey Richie, look what I have here," Bob said, holding up the tube of heat rub.

Richie stopped beating Dominick with the back brush, looked at Bob, and the two men cracked up loudly with laughter. Dominick was standing with his head hanging down, his sweat soaked hair dangling in his face, looking down at the sink and his cock lying on the vanity. He was snuffling and grunting uncontrollably, his huge male cleavage heaving up and down as he took deep breath after deep breath. He was wondering just what the fuck kind of buddies Richie and Bob were that they could do these things to him.

"Oh man, is he in for it now," Richie said, sounding almost like he felt sorry for Dominick, but not quite. "Okay Dominick old buddy, spread those legs apart again for us..."

With no choice other than to do as he was told Dominick spread his legs, exposing his asshole for his two buddies perverse pleasures.

"It's your call..." Richie said to Bob.

Bob squeezed a good amount of the heat rub onto his fingers then rammed his fingers into Dominick's hole.

"AAAARHHHH!!" Dominick gasped, practically jumping out of his socks.

Bob worked his fingers meanly around in Dominick's hole, really working the heat rub in there. Seconds later Dominick was burning up back there like crazy. His two buddies watched intently as he hopped around the bathroom in burning and excruciating pain, screaming his head off. When the heat rub in his hole eventually wore off Bob quickly squeezed some more out of the tube and jammed his fingers up in Dominick's asshole again, getting him hopping and dancing all over again. The two men laughed hysterically at Dominick as he screamed in agony, a look of insanity beginning to creep into his features. The second time the heat rub wore off they didn't put anymore of it up Dominick's ass. Instead, they bent him over the sink and rubbed a good amount of it over his bound and swollen balls, really squeezing his poor balls as they did their dirty work.

"OHHHRRRRRR!!!" Dominick roared, looking down pitifully into the sink.

"Work it over his balls real good," Richie said. "I want to see him dance again."

He didn't have to wait long because once Dominick's balls were smeared with the heat rub he was hopping and dancing around like mad all over again. After a few more minutes Dominick was sweating like a pig all over again and smelling really bad. Actually, he smelled like a rancid mixture of piss, sweat, beer, and of course the heat rub. When the heat rub all over his balls wore off a good while later he propped himself up against a cold tile wall, heaving and gasping for breath, wanting for all of this to be over already…but inwardly he knew that

Richie and Bob did not plan to let up on him for a while yet...a long while. As he stood there trying desperately to catch his breath his two buddies rubbed some of the heat rub onto his sore nipples, really squeezing them in the process to get the stuff worked in.

"OHHHHRRRRR no, no..." Dominick screeched as his nipples came to burning life.

He clenched his teeth and doubled over in agony anew. As he stood there hunched over Richie grabbed the back brush and beat him again on his upper muscular arms, his ass cheeks and the backs of his thighs. The sound of the brush as it connected with skin was maddening in Dominick's ears. Dominick screamed in anger and pain all over again. He knew that by the next day he would be severely bruised and wondered if he would be able to report for work come Monday morning. He stupidly thought how it seemed like flames would fan out of his nipples; they felt that hot, like they were on fire. Finally, the heat rub wore off his nipples and instead of applying more of it his two buddies each soaked a washcloth with cold water. They wiped the heat rub off his balls and nipples and delighted in hearing his shouts of pain as they wiped out his asshole as they really dug deep in there.

"I think we'd better give him a break at this point," Richie said to Bob. "We don't want him dropping dead on us after all."

"Yeah, I agree with you on that," Bob said. "The poor fuck looks exhausted."

"Well, its only going to be a short break and then we'll put the screws to him again...and believe me I have some stuff planned that'll make what we've done to him so far seem like a damned warm-up."

Dominick looked at Richie in disbelief, praying that he was kidding...although he knew he wasn't.

"Come on, lets take him to the bedroom," Richie said. "We can stretch him out on my bed for a while."

Dominick's two buddies again took him by an arm and leg each and carried him out of the bathroom. In the bedroom they untied him...finally...only to quickly re-tie him (this time at the wrists and ankles) to the bed in a spread eagle position. (For the moment that Dominick had been untied he didn't even attempt to get away from his two buddies as they had quickly grabbed his muscular arms and pulled them far apart to get him roped to the bed. He was feeling too numb in spots and too damned tired to even try anything. He also knew that if he did try to get away from them and failed that there would be hell to pay for it. Best to just keep going along with this awful game he figured.) They however did not bother to untie his poor aching balls. They left them bound and they were very swollen looking, trapped under his ass crack. Before tying Dominick's feet to the ends of the bed Richie pulled my roommate's sweat socks off his feet and stuffed each of them into a different pocket of his jeans.

"Oh man, now you really got me totally naked here bud," Dominick said forlornly. "Fucker just took off my last two pieces of modesty here..."

"What the fuck are you doin' with his socks man?" Bob asked Richie as he sat on the bed at Dominick's side, toying with one of his nipples, looking lustfully at his very exposed, very hairy armpits.

"Keepin' them as souvenirs of all this," Richie responded. "Lets face it; he's never going to let us do this shit to him again. You can have his briefs if you want..."

As the two men spoke to each other about keeping Dominick's socks and briefs as souvenirs his cock grew hard and stiff. He was glad in a way because he knew it was alright after the open palmed whapping they had given it earlier.

"Man, his feet sure do stink," Richie said as he finished roping one of Dominick's big feet to the leg of the bed. "Come here Bob, take a good hearty sniff of this foot odor of his..."

Bob let go of Dominick's nipple that he had been toying with (almost reluctantly), tore his eyes away from Dominick's bushy armpit (almost reluctantly) and squatted with Richie at one of his bound and smelly feet.

"Oh man you're right," Bob said agreeably after taking a deep sniff of Dominick's foot. "Stinks like all hell..."

"Yeah, but at the same time it's kind of inviting you know," Richie said, grabbed the top of Dominick's foot by the toes section and ran his tongue over the bottom of Dominick's beefy foot.

"Oh man, I can't believe that you just did that," Bob said to Richie in disbelief.

"Neither can I," Dominick piped up as he squirmed in the tight bondage.

"Try it man..."Richie said and took another hearty lick at the bottom of Dominick's bound foot.

"I don't know man, its one thing to work a guy over for the fun of it and see how much he can take, but to lick at his mangy feet..." Bob said, sounding unsure of what Richie was suggesting, yet at the same time looking curiously at Dominick's big, smelly and bound foot.

Bob had to admit that there truly was something about the way that big foot looked with the ropes tied around it and snagged off to the leg of the bed, keeping his good buddy totally at their mercy.

"Try it man!!" Richie said sternly, reminding Bob of just who was in charge. "It's not like he can do anything to stop you. The way we have this poor fuck tied up we can do whatever the fuck we want to him."

Richie reluctantly stuck out his tongue and took a long slurp at the bottom of Dominick's foot. He looked at Richie, smiled, and quickly licked Dominick's foot a second and then a third time.

"Look at you man, fucking look at you, you like it more than me," Richie chortled loudly. "You love licking his smelly god-damned feet!"

Dominick lifted his head up off the bed and looked down at his two buddies taking turns licking the bottom of one of his meaty feet that they were squatting at.

"Oh man, I really do not believe this shit…" Dominick said with a grin, chills of delight coursing through his muscular body his two buddies licked and licked his foot. "You perverts, you sleazy bastards…just look at the two of you licking and slurping my damned smelly foot…"

Dominick laid his head back down and enjoyed the feeling coursing through him as his two buddies ran their tongues up and down the sides of his foot, over the bottom of it again, and they even sucked his toes a few times each. At one point Richie was licking the bottom of Dominick's foot as Bob dribbled saliva over the top of it and quickly slurped it up.

"OHHHHHH man, I do have to admit, that does feel fucking great," Dominick murmured.

Dominick reveled in the wonderful feeling of his two buddies licking his foot because he knew that it was only a short reprieve…and he knew that soon they would be torturing the shit out of him again… When they moved over to his other foot and began licking that one he lifted his muscular torso off the bed in sheer ecstasy. His cock, all purple at the tip and feeling sort of achy was hard as a rock. It had to be the most painful erection he had ever had. His balls, damn, his poor balls were aching yet throbbing underneath him.

"Ohhhhh man, you fucking guys are making me crazy…" Dominick crooned as they tongued his other foot like mad.

"Glad you like it so much asshole…" Richie said. "Because you're not going to fucking believe what I have planned for you next…"

At the sound of that threat Dominick laid his sexy body back down on the bed, looked up at the ceiling, and gulped hard in terror. When they finally stopped feasting on his rancid feet Richie looked at the steely erection that Dominick was sporting between his tree-trunk like legs.

"Like having your smelly feet licked eh buddy boy?" Richie asked his bound up friend and grabbed Dominick's hard throbbing cock in hand and gave it a tight squeeze.

"AAARRHHHH fuck man, easy with my cock huh?" Dominick pleaded.

Richie gave Dominick's cock a few good strokes and he shot another good sized load of ball juice, all over his chest this time.

"OOOHHHRRRR shit man, got me creamin' like crazy again," Dominick panted wildly and bucked on the bed. "OHHHHHH fuck yeah…"

When Dominick was done shooting his load Richie let go of his cock and gave it a few hard slaps as it went soft and shrively.

"AAAAARRHHHHHHH!!! FUCKER MAN!!!" Dominick ranted at him through clenched teeth. "That's a real fucked up thing to do to a poor guy's cock after he's just shot his sexy load man…"

"Hey Richie," Bob began. "I just came up with a great fucking idea. Lets get him off the bed and to his feet again…"
They untied Dominick's feet from the bed first and then untied his wrists. They each quickly grabbed Dominick by one wrist each and hauled him roughly off the bed and up to his bare feet. When they had their captive buddy standing between them they meanly yanked his arms back up behind him.

"AAAARHHHHHH easy you guys…" Dominick moaned.

"Don't want you getting any ideas you prick," Richie said. "I see it in your eyes man. I know that if you had the chance you would be out of here. Shit, I would be…"

A few minutes later Dominick was standing with his arms crossed up behind himself all roped up like he had been earlier. Richie brought him a glass of cold water from the bathroom and held it to Dominick's trembling lips. Dominick sipped it down gratefully. After the piss he had drank earlier he was very happy to be drinking fresh cold water.

"There you go buddy boy," Richie said as Dominick drank the cold water. "Don't want you dehydrating on us after all."

When Dominick was done with the water Richie put the glass back in the bathroom and then asked Bob what his idea was. Bob smiled wickedly, walked over to Richie's clothes closet, opened it, and took two unused wire hangers off the clothes pole. Richie clapped his hands together, laughed hysterically, and took one of the wire hangers from Bob.

"That is such a fucking Joan Crawford idea!!" Richie said to Bob and rubbed the wire hanger he was holding against Dominick's muscular chest, under and over his huge male cleavage and over his sore jutted up nipples.

"Don't you guys think you beat on me enough earlier?" Dominick asked meekly and Richie whacked him hard across the chest with the wire hanger. "Yowwwwwccchhhhh!!!"

"One good beating always deserves another ol' buddy," Richie snickered and whacked Dominick again across the chest, making sure to connect with his sore nipples.

"YOOWWWWW!! BASTARDS!!" Dominick ranted through clenched teeth.

Bob hooked a hand around one of Dominick's biceps, his hand not quite making it all the way around and Richie grabbed the poor guy's other biceps. Holding Dominick steady between themselves they proceeded to really whale into the guy's big chest with those wire hangers. Dominick screamed in pain and agony as they whapped and walloped the tar out of his iron-like chest, purposely aiming for his sore nipples. His nipples had already endured so much torture that he wondered just how much more they could take... His two buddies were aiming to find out it seemed. In moments Dominick's nipples were horribly,

horribly swollen all over again. The sound of the wire hangers connecting with his chest was maddening and the pain he felt each time was even worse. His buddies held him tight and beat on his pecs a few times. Then, Richie rubbed his wire hanger across Dominick's stomach, told him to stand at soldierly attention and to tighten up his abs area. Dominick took a deep breath and did as Richie said. Laughing, cackling, and having a grand ol' time his two buddies whapped the shit out of his flat stomach till it was red and good and striped.

Dominick grunted miserably each time those wire hangers connected with his flat stomach. He did his best to remain standing at attention as his buddies' whapped and walloped his stomach, him almost doubling over in pain a few times. Finally, after what seemed like hundreds of hard whacks and whaps they stopped beating his stomach and Richie told him to bend the fuck over. Again Dominick did as he was told and the men rubbed the wire hangers over his already very red ass cheeks.

"Man, I never thought I would enjoy all this as much as I am," Bob said to Richie. "His poor ass cheeks are going to look and feel even worse after this…"

"No shit man, just be careful of his nuts," Richie said, pointing out Dominick's swollen balls that were still tied and sticking out under his ass crack. "We're just having some sadistic fun with him, we don't want him winding up in the hospital…"

Then, holding Dominick's arms tight in their grasps with his body slightly bent over and his ass sticking up real sexily, his two buddies gave his ass cheeks a good hard beating with the wire hangers. They alternated swishing the wire hangers up and down and bringing them down hard on the poor guy's upturned butt cheeks.

"OOOHHRRRRRRR!!!" Dominick roared like a bear with

its foot caught in a trap.

They whacked his ass cheeks over and over and over with those wire hangers. When they stopped a while later Dominick straightened up and stood there with tears rolling down his cheeks, shaking like a leaf, and wondering just how much more he would be able to endure. It had begun more than a couple of hours ago and he didn't see any relief in sight...not anytime soon... His two buddies tossed their wire hangers on the bed and rubbed their hands over Dominick's chest, his broad shoulders and upper arms.

"Easy buddy, easy," Richie said to Dominick soothingly. "You're doing great...so far..."

Dominick looked at him miserably as he and Bob squeezed his swollen nipples and even twisted them a few times. It seemed that they truly delighted in torturing his nipples more than anything else.

"I'm hungry..." Dominick said softly.

"Yeah, me too," Richie said, holding one of Dominick's nipples between his thumb and first finger, squeezing it. "I did invite you guys here for lunch after all."

Richie seemed to mull it over for a few seconds and then looked at Dominick.

"Tell you what buddy boy, I want to work you over in the basement for a while, then we'll eat," Richie said. "That okay with you Bob?"

"Fine with me," Bob said. "I can wait till tomorrow to eat. I just want to see what the fuck you have planned for him down in the basement..."

"He isn't going to like it, that's for sure," Richie said and he and Bob laughed hysterically.

"Shit..." Dominick whispered.

"Come on Dom, lead the way to the basement," Richie ordered and gave one of Dominick's ass cheeks a squeeze, jiggling it a bit before letting go.

Dominick walked out of Richie's bedroom, down the stairs, through the living room, toward the basement stairs. As they walked through the kitchen Dominick realized that he smelled pretty damn bad at the moment, a mixture of sweat, piss, cum and beer and not to mention the heat rub that his two buddies had slathered on him and in him. Shit, but he felt and smelled like a disaster. When they got to the basement Dominick saw that Richie had a large collection of exercise machines, including a weight bench with a bar set up above it.
"Ready to workout buddy boy?" Richie asked Dominick and began untying him.

Like earlier he left Dominick's balls tied. My roommate somehow knew better than to reach down and untie his most private of areas. Moments later Dominick was lying on his muscular and ripped back on the bench and hefting the weight bar up and down over his massive chest. Richie had placed ninety pounds worth of weights on the bar and by the seventh rep Dominick was beginning to falter. Bob was standing behind Dominick spotting him as Richie squatted at his tied balls, squeezing the fuck out of them, tugging meanly on them, and even snapping his fingers against them.

"AAAARGGGHHHHH!!" Dominick roared from the pain Richie was inflicting on his poor balls and the chore of hefting that heavy weight bar.

As he brought the weight bar down toward his chest on the tenth rep he knew that he would not be able to heft it back up again.

"OOHHHRRRR shit..." Dominick gasped. "Bob, help me man, I-I can't lift the fucking thing up!!"

As Bob was about to grab the weight bar from Dominick Richie gave his balls a hard slap. Dominick screamed in agony, sweated like crazy, and held the weight bar rigidly over his chest.

"Don't touch that weight bar Bob!!" Richie shouted and gave Dominick's balls a hard squeeze. "Come on fucker, lift that shit!! I know you have it in you to do it!!"

Dominick roared like an angry animal and lifted the bar up, then repeated the motion again.

Fuck man, complaining like that is going to cost you Dominick," Richie said and slapped Dominick's balls again, getting another loud scream out of him. "Big fucking time..."

With his teeth clenched and sweat dripping all over himself Dominick looked down at Richie angrily as he continued toying with his bound balls.

"Fucker!!" Dominick screeched at him.

After a total of sixteen excruciatingly hard reps they allowed Dominick to stop. Bob placed the weight bar back on the rack and Dominick sat up on the bench, heaving and gasping for breath. Once he was breathing evenly his two buddies brought him over to a leg press machine. Richie set the weight at one hundred pounds and told Dominick to get busy. Dominick sat up on the seat of the machine, placed his ankles behind the bar that worked the weights and began the exercise, pushing the bar with his naked feet. He grunted and groaned like a madman, wanting all of this to be over once and for all. But he knew that was still a long way in coming.

"Hey Bob, I have another idea," Richie said and dashed over to a wooden cabinet on the wall.

Richie came back holding two round leather paddles in his hand. He handed one to Bob. Bob smiled wickedly and he and Richie stood at Dominick's sides. Richie raised his paddle and brought it down hard on Dominick's nipple which was closest to him.

"YOOWWWWCCCHHHH!!" Dominick screeched loudly and Bob pummeled his other nipple. "EEEEEEERRRRHHH!!!"

As Dominick worked his legs past exhaustion his two buddies whapped his sore nipples over and over and over, harder and harder each time with those damned leather paddles.

""G-guys...please..." Dominick gasped as he continued to work his legs and have his nipples beaten at the same time. "AAAARRRRHHHH!!!"

When his nipples were very smashed and very red and sore the two men stopped beating them. Richie told Dominick to do five more reps on the leg press machine and then to stretch his legs. All totaled Dominick had done fifty painful reps on that machine. When he was done he hopped off it and bent over to stretch his numbed legs and thighs. His two buddies saw their golden opportunity and went for it. As Dominick was bent over stretching out his legs they gave his upturned ass cheeks a few hard whacks with their leather paddles.

"YOWWWCCHHHH!!!" Dominick bellowed. "No rest for the weary eh guys?"

He finished stretching out his legs and stood up straight. He turned to Richie, raised a shaking finger and looked at him squarely in the eyes.

"Let me tell you something, buddy..." Dominick said breathlessly, standing there worked over and naked, stinking like crazy, totally angry and humiliated. "If you had lost that fucking card game I wouldn't be so damned sadistic with you...just wanted you to know that bud..."

"That's because you aren't as creative as me..." Richie said, looking at Dominick fiendishly. "...buddy..."

Moments passed and then Dominick was standing in the center of the basement with a long weight bar strewn across his broad and muscular shoulders. Richie and Bob were placing ten pound weights at the ends of the weight bar as Dominick stood there trying to keep the bar steady on his big construction worker shoulders, gripping it tightly as the weight on it increased and increased. As he balanced the bar his head spun and for some reason he didn't even remember how the bar had come to be across his shoulders.

"Okay buddy boy, I told you that you were going to pay big time for complaining," Richie said and added another ten pound round weight to the bar. "Well, here it is, and believe me this isn't going to be easy by a long shot..."

When there was a total of one hundred and twenty pounds on the bar Dominick clenched his teeth, gripped the bar tighter, and did his very best to stay on his feet as the weight pressed down on him.

"Ohhhhhhhrrrrr GOD..." Dominick gasped throatily.

From the way Bob was looking at Dominick he could tell that his buddy was feeling a little sorry for him at that point.

"Hey Richie, do you think that's enough weight on there?" Bob asked as Richie added yet another twenty pounds to the bar.

"Nah, he can handle it," Richie said. "On the job I've seen him lift even heavier than this."

Dominick looked at Bob miserably as Richie placed another ten pounds on the bar. Sweat dripped from his forehead down into his eyes, irritating the fuck out of him. He was dizzy and thinking he was about to pass out. Finally, when there was one hundred and fifty pounds on the bar Richie stopped adding weight. Dominick stood there with that awful weight across his shoulders as his two buddies stood in front of him...yanking hairs out of his chest, in his stomach area, and even pubic hairs from his crotch.

"UUUUHHRRRRRRRR!!!" Dominick ranted and moaned miserably.

"Hey Dom, how about another game of cards next weekend?" Richie asked Dominick mockingly and yanked out a few more of his curly pubic hairs.

"OOOOOORRRRRRRR!!!!!" Dominick cried.

"Man, that has to fucking hurt," Bob said and yanked out a few of Dominick's chest hairs.

"Wh-why the fuck would I want to do that?" Dominick gasped.

"Who knows, maybe you would win," Richie said just as mockingly and pulled out a few more of Dominick's chest hairs. "Then again, maybe you'll lose again and Bob and I would have to work you over all over again..."

"R-Richie...pl-please man..." Dominick gasped. "Fun's fun but this weight is fucking killing me!!"

"A few more minutes buddy then we'll get that shit off your shoulders..." Richie said and squeezed one of Dominick's nipples hard.

A few minutes can seem like a few hours to someone in the position that Dominick was in, but finally his two buddies lifted the weight bar off his shoulders. He stood there bent over again with his hands on his knees as they put the weight bar down on the floor.

"God almighty..." Dominick whispered hoarsely.

Then, he found himself laying on the bench on his stomach, his hands roped together at the wrists under the bench, his feet pulled wide apart and tied off at the ankles to weights positioned on the floor, and his tied balls and cock pulled under his exposed ass crack.

"FUCKING fucks man, guys got me tied up again, I thought we were at least done with that shit!!" Dominick complained bitterly.

Richie had found an old smelly and very used jockstrap on the floor and crammed it in Dominick's mouth, gagging him. Dominick's eyes rolled in his head as the taste of Richie's piss and sweat assaulted his taste buds. Richie and Bob were now taking turns whacking Dominick's ass cheeks over and over with their leather paddles as he lay trapped on the bench.

"RRRRMMMFFFF!!!" Dominick sputtered wildly and squirmed helplessly on the bench.

They really laid into the poor guy at one point, rapping him so hard on the butt that he thought he was going to start bleeding. But Richie was super careful about that and about not accidentally rapping Dominick's balls with the paddles. Finally, they decided that Dominick had had enough and his two buddies rubbed a good amount of soothing aloe cream all over his poor stinging ass cheeks. They stuck their fingers into his mangy hole a few times and prodded it. Dominick felt like they were digging for gold in his shit chute. They untied him, took the foul tasting jockstrap out of his mouth, and helped the poor battered guy to his feet. Dominick stood there wobbling with his balls still tied as his two buddies tweaked his nipples a few times each.

"Man, he really looks all beat to shit..." Bob commented. "Maybe we should let him have some lunch and be done with it. What do you think Richie?"

"I think not Bob old boy," Richie said and squeezed one of Dominick's pecs hard. "I think our buddy here can handle a lot more...but in the meantime, let's go have some lunch..."

"Who the fuck can eat at a time like this?" Dominick whispered.

Upstairs in the kitchen they all sat around the table eating cold-cut sandwiches, pickles, coleslaw, and drinking soda. Dominick sat there quietly much of the time, totally naked, his balls tied and aching. He was wondering just how straight these two buddies of his really were. After all, he had to face the fact that throughout torturing him they had sucked his nipples, (he had to admit to himself how much he loved that) they had sucked his cock, forced him to shoot his load a few times, and even licked and sucked his rancid and stinking feet. Was all of this a ploy so that they could get their mangy hands and other parts of them on him?

"Feeling okay Dominick?" Bob asked him, startling the guy away from his very private thoughts.

"Yeah, great, just great," Dominick replied softly, looking at Bob miserably. "I just love having the shit beat out of me by my two best buddies in the whole fucking world..."

"Yeah, it's a bitch all right, but you sure as shit can take it Dominick," Richie said and clapped Dominick hard on the back.

Dominick gulped his soda and poured himself some more. After eating two and a half good sized sandwiches and drinking two full glasses of soda he was pretty much full. He sat back in his chair, his cock semi hard and looked at Richie.

"So what else do you bastards have up your sleeves?" Dominick asked Richie.

"Anxious to get started again Dominick?" Richie asked in reply.

"I just want it to be over-with already man..." Dominick replied sheepishly

Richie looked up at the clock on the wall, saw that it was just after three o'clock in the afternoon, and looked back at Dominick.

"You've got hours and hours to go yet my friend..." Richie said. "That's the price that the loser of the card game pays after all..."

Dominick leaned back in his chair and hung his head down…he had all to do to keep his tears from flowing… When lunch was over Richie made Dominick get up on the table with his knees tucked under him and his hairy sexy ass way up in the air. He had tied Dominick's hands at the wrists in front of him as Bob stood behind my roommate and roped his feet together.

"What are we going to do to him now?" Bob asked anxiously, giving one of Dominick's moist and smelly feet a squeeze.

Smiling, Richie opened a cabinet and took out two long candles. He and Bob laughed as Dominick looked at the candles despondently. The poor lug didn't need three guesses to know what the fuck was coming next. The two men lit the candles and began dripping the hot melted wax all over Dominick's wounded ass cheeks, slapping his ass cheeks in between dripping the wax on them.

"YOWWWWWW!!!" Dominick cried out loudly as the wax dripped on his cheeks and down onto his thighs.

They flipped Dominick onto his back then and dripped candle wax onto his chest as well; his stomach and even in his mangy and sweaty armpits.

"AAAARHHHHHHHHH you fuckers!!" Dominick ranted wildly.

His tied feet were dangling off the end of the table and as Richie dripped candle wax on his jutted up nipples Dominick suddenly felt a tongue lapping at them. He lifted his head up, looked down at the end of the table and saw that Bob was happily licking the bottoms and sides of his feet alternately.
"Oh man, that fucking guy is licking my damned feet again!"

Dominick said to Richie.

"Yeah, it sure as fuck looks like Bob loves those big stinkers of yours huh buddy boy?" Richie asked Dominick mockingly and dripped hot candle wax again onto Dominick's nipples.

"YOWWWWWW!!!" Dominick screamed.

When Bob was done licking Dominick's feet he held a lit candle over Dominick's fear hard and throbbing cock. He dripped wax onto the shaft of it and even into the tip of it. Dominick screamed wildly in sheer agony and bucked like crazy in the tight bondage atop the table…

An hour or so later the two men blew out the candles and Dominick was literally slathered in wax. They had dripped the shit practically all over him and he was feeling totally awful at the moment… He didn't want to think about how the hell he was going to get all that damned melted wax off himself later on.

Richie and Bob then hoisted my roommate off the table and stood him on his bound feet.

"What's next Richie?" Bob asked.

"First lets get him roped up the way he was before," Richie said and began untying Dominick's hands. "I like it better when his hands and arms are roped up behind him…"

When his hands and feet were untied Dominick thought about bolting the fuck out of there, but he didn't want to appear to be a wussy after all. Besides, his hands didn't remain untied all that long. Richie and Bob quickly grabbed his wrists and yanked his muscular arms up behind him and again roped them together in three places, real good and fucking tight. Once again they wound rope over and under his shoulders and tied the slack of it to his bound up arms, keeping them way up behind him. Dominick looked down at himself and a feeling of utter and total misery coursed through him. He was feeling totally defeated and totally enslaved, yeah, that was the word for how he was feeling, enslaved.

"God..." Dominick said to himself, feeling that his whole life had all come down to this horror-filled experience and at the hands of his two buddies at that.

His cock was hard as a rock and his bound balls were aching like he could not believe...

"Not feeling all that good eh buddy boy?" Richie asked Dominick contemptuously, his hand on Dominick's shoulder. Dominick simply nodded his head "no", not even bothering to give Richie the benefit of a spoken reply.

"Well then, with what's coming next you're going to be feeling lots worse..." Richie said with a wicked grin on his face and he squeezed Dominick's shoulder harder, getting a loud whimper out of him.

Then, with no warning whatsoever, Richie grabbed the topmost part of Dominick's cock in his hand, closed his fist around the tip of it so that the tip of it was sticking out of his fist, and with his other hand whapped the crown of Dominick's manhood with his palm.

"AAAYYYYYYY!!!" Dominick screamed loudly and began hopping around in agony anew as Richie whapped the tip of his cock again. "AAAYYYYYRRRRRRR!!!!"

"Damn Richie, that is an awful fucking thing to do to the poor lug," Bob said, stepping next to Richie. "Hold that cock of his tight. Let me give it a shot or two..."

Dominick nodded his head "NO" furiously back and forth like a madman, tears streaming freely down his cheeks, silently begging his friend not to whap his poor cock, but like Richie, Bob showed him no mercy.

"Please man, that's my goddamned cock he has in his fist," Dominick managed to blubber.

Bob raised his hand high and brought it down open palmed on the very tip of Dominick's poor aching cock.

"AYYYYYRRRRR!!!" Dominick roared in misery and hopped around stupidly in place as Riche continued to hold tight to his cock.

"Heh, heh, lookit the poor fucker dance," Richie said and Bob whapped Dominick's cock two more times.

"AAAAAYYYRRRRR!!!' Dominick bellowed uncontrollably.

Richie let go of Dominick's cock when it was evident that it could not take another whap anytime soon. The tip of his cock was numb, tingling from within and tinted a horrible mixture of red and purple. Dominick stood there doubled over in agony, crying and sniveling like crazy, his sweat soaked hair hanging messily in his face, and snot dripping from his nostrils and into his mouth.

"AAAAYYYYYY GOD, fucking bastards," Dominick screeched, looking at his wounded cock through his tears. "My cock, my poor fucking cock..."

"Yeah, it sure is taking a beating," Richie quipped and took Dominick by his arm. "Come on Bob, we're taking our good buddy here back up to the bathroom. I just got another fucking fiendish brainstorm."

"Is there no end to your evil imagination?" Bob asked Richie as he followed him and Dominick up the stairs.

Richie held Dominick tightly by his upper arm as he walked him slowly up the stairs. Dominick didn't have any idea of what Richie had in mind for him next but whatever the fuck it was he was dreading it already. In the bathroom Richie left Dominick alone with Bob for a few moments while he dashed to a hall cabinet to get what they would need for the next round of torturing my roommate. Bob took a long strand of toilet paper off the role and gently wiped the tears, sweat and snot off Dominick's handsome face for him.

"Th-thank you…" Dominick whispered.

"Yeah, you're welcome buddy," Bob said and tossed the toilet paper in the wastebasket, looking at Dominick almost sorrowfully. "You okay?"

Dominick nodded "Yes" and then "No" and then Bob put his hands gently behind Dominick's neck. He leaned in close to Dominick and with a look of uncertainty etched on his face he kissed Dominick softly on the lips. Dominick didn't say a word or change the expression on his face as Bob caressed the back of his bull-sized neck.

"If that makes me a faggot so be it…" Bob said softly. "You are one hell of a fucking sport buddy…"

Bob kissed Dominick again on the lips and then took his hands off Dominick's neck. Just then Richie came back into the bathroom.

"Okay Dominick, are you ready for this shit?" Richie asked and held up two long straight pins.

"Oh shit, what are those for?" Bob asked Richie.

"Suck one of his tasty titties till it's nice and erect and I'll be glad to show you…" Richie said with a shit eating grin on his face.

They pushed Dominick up against a wall and went to work vigorously sucking on his sore nipples like two bitches in heat.

"AAARRRHHHHH shhhiiittt…" Dominick gasped wildly as his cock grew again painfully hard between his muscular legs. "Ohhhhh you fuckers…"

As they sucked his nipples he did not need three guesses to know what the long straight pins were going to be used for. About ten minutes or so later they stopped working Dominick's nipples. They were fully erect, swollen, and pointy on his chest like two small bullets. His buddies rubbed them and squeezed them between their fingers to feel their hardness and texture and then Richie declared that it was time. He handed one of the straight pins to Bob.

"Oh God you guys, don't, please don't…" Dominick whispered in anguish.

Bob watched as Richie pressed the tip of his needle against the side of Dominick's sore and swollen right nipple. "Oh shit Richie," Bob said and instantly did the same thing to Dominick's left nipple with his needle.

"AAYYYYRRRRR…" Dominick screeched through clenched teeth as his two buddies pushed their needles through the tips of his nipples. "OHHHRRRRRR…"

Dominick's loud screams of pain echoed off the tile walls of the bathroom and Richie and Bob stepped away from him to admire their handiwork.

"Shit Richie, he's in total fucking agony..." Bob said, looking slightly concerned.

"Not totally just yet..." Richie said and took two lengths of thin string out of his pocket and handed Bob one of them. "What's the string for?" Bob asked.

"Watch..." Richie said intently and picked up a half full tube of toothpaste from the vanity.

Bob watched (and Dominick watched as well, but in silent agony with his teeth clenched) as Richie tied the string around and under the cap of the tube of the toothpaste. Then, Richie squatted in front of Dominick and tied the slack of the string around one of my roommate's bound and aching balls.

"EEEEEHHHHRRRRR NO, no..." Dominick ranted hoarsely, knowing all too well what was going to happen next. "Oh God man, my balls, my poor balls..."

"Okay Bob, watch what happens when I let go of this tube of toothpaste," Richie said, holding the tube of toothpaste in his hand.

"I fucking shudder to even think about it..." Bob said, looking at Dominick in amazement.

"No, no..." Dominick whispered miserably. "Oh God please no, Richie..."

Richie let go of the tube of toothpaste, it plummeted

toward the floor, and stopped in midair, yanking Dominick's nut that it was tied to intensely. Dominick screamed so fucking loud that Bob had to put his hand over his mouth to stifle the noise that Dominick was making. Bob held one hand over Dominick's mouth and his other hand behind Dominick's neck as Richie hoisted the tube of toothpaste again, prepared to jar Dominick's tied nut again. Dominick was again crying and sniveling uncontrollably, screaming the word "NO" over and over again against Bob's hand over his mouth. Richie let go of the tube of toothpaste and Dominick screamed again in bloody again.

"Okay Bob, tie the string I gave you around that tube of toothpaste on the vanity and then tie it off to his other nut," Richie instructed his buddy. "We'll jar his nuts at the same time and really get him screeching."

With a look on his face that seemed to be saying "I'm sorry" Bob did as Richie had instructed him to do. Dominick stood there with his lips trembling and tears upon tears streaming down his face as his two buddies each held a tube of toothpaste in their hands…tubes of toothpaste that were tied to his poor swollen, aching, throbbing and very wounded balls.

"Okay, on three…" Richie said to Bob as they squatted in front of Dominick.

"Okay, but only once Richie," Bob said sternly. "His balls aren't looking all that great right now."

"Okay, just once," Richie said grudgingly. "One, two…"

Dominick clenched his teeth, prepared for the inevitable jolt of pain that was going to sear through him.

"…three…" Richie said and he and Bob released their holds on their tubes of toothpaste.

The two tubes plummeted toward the floor and before reaching it they stopped midway, yanking Dominick's balls miserably.

"AAAAYYYRRRRRR!!!" he roared, his voice again echoing off the walls of the bathroom.

When he was about to double over in pain Richie straightened him up and squeezed his pierced nipples hard.

"AAAARHHHHHH!!!!" Dominick ranted in pure agony, looking at Richie through his tears.

"Now he's in total agony," Richie said to Bob with a smirk on his face.

Dominick's two buddies watched him writhe in total agony as he stood there against the cold tile wall in the bathroom with his nipples pierced and his balls tied with two tubes of toothpaste dangling off them.

"Amazing what you can do to a guy with average everyday household items…" Richie mused, looking at the two tubes of toothpaste hanging on Dominick's balls.

They left him that way for a good fifteen minutes (maybe more) and then Richie told Bob to get busy taking the tube of toothpaste off one of his nuts while he did the honors of removing the other one. When they were done taking the tubes of toothpaste off Dominick's balls they then removed the pins from his nipples. Tiny spurts of blood formed on the tips of Dominick's nips.

"Th-thank you…" Dominick whimpered and Richie smoothed his hair back away from his handsome face for him.

"You're welcome buddy," Richie said and squeezed the back of Dominick's neck.

Then, Richie pulled the shower curtain back and told Dominick to step into the tub. Dominick looked at him quizzically and simply did as he was told and stepped into the tub. Richie told Dominick to turn his back to him and Bob.

"What do you have in mind now Richie?" Bob asked.

"Something that I cannot stand..."Richie replied. "I hate it when a guy snaps a wet towel against my damned naked butt in a locker room...you know, even if he's just clowning around after a hard workout or a good ball game..."

Dominick heaved a loud sigh of frustration as Richie grabbed a towel off the rack and soaked it with warm water in the sink. Bob, laughing, also grabbed a towel and soaked it as well.

"Okay, give it to him as hard as possible," Richie said, rolling up his wet towel real tight. "It's only a towel you're hitting him with after all...on his very wounded, very red, and very hurting ass cheeks."

"Count on it man," Bob said.

They took turns swiping Dominick's naked butt cheeks good and fucking hard with their wet towels. Each swipe stung more than the one before it. Dominick tried his best to stand still and endure the shit that his two buddies were heaping on him. After a good twenty to thirty swipes Richie ordered Dominick to spread his legs and bend over. He turned his head, looked at Richie miserably, and again did as he was told. His balls were now a ready target for them. Richie went first, swiping Dominick's balls good and hard with his rolled up wet towel, followed quickly by Bob. That got a few real good and loud screams out of Dominick and made his poor tortured balls swell up even more. If Dominick's balls could talk they would have asked him if he had gone crazy and why was he heaping so much abuse on them. Dominick leaned over further with his head pressed against the wall as his two buddies swiped his ass cheeks and tied balls over and over with the wet towels. By the time they stopped (a good while later actually) Dominick was heaving for breath once again, crying profusely, and needing to piss real badly.

"Okay, I think he's had enough of that," Richie said and he and Bob hung their towels over the shower rod to dry. "Man, I have to piss."

"Me too man," Bob said.

When Dominick straightened up and turned around he was shocked to see his two buddies standing there with their big fat cocks sticking out of their pants. They each held their cock pointed at Dominick and they pissed on him, aiming for his chest, his legs, his nest of pubic hair, and his cock. When Dominick pissed it landed all over his chest. Some of it even landed on his face because his cock was sticking straight up. It still stung like hell as Dominick pissed because of the liquid soap that Richie had poured in his piss slit earlier. But Dominick found at that moment that there's no worse feeling in the world than having your two best buddies in the world piss on you…literally. The bathtub reeked of sour piss and so did my roommate. When they were done Dominick was really smelling real fucking raunchy and ripe. He was wishing Richie would turn on the shower and rinse him off a bit (a lot?) but instead the sadistic guy ordered Dominick to his knees in the tub. Dominick looked questioningly at him and Bob. Seconds later Dominick was on his knees facing his two buddies as they dangled their big cocks in his face.

"Suck 'em buddy boy..." Richie said sternly.

"Oh shit, you're actually going to make him suck our cocks Richie?" Bob asked in amazement, trying not to show that this was something he had been hoping to have happen.

"Sure, why the fuck not?" Richie asked in reply. "It doesn't make him a faggot or anything, its just one of those things that a loser has to do...and if he doesn't we'll teach him a lesson he won't soon forget..."

Seeing as Richie was being and had been a total prick all along Dominick decided to make him wait. It was the first feeling of some kind of control that he had since it had all begun hours ago. He leaned forward and slurped Bob's semi hard cock into his mouth.

"OHHHHHH shit Richie, OHHHHH God," Bob sputtered and bucked his body back and forth. "Fucking guy is actually doin' it...look at him sucking my damned cock...God but it feels great too man!!"

Richie looked at Dominick in amazement as he sucked Bob's cock for all he was worth. It wasn't really Dominick's idea of fun to be sucking Bob's awful tasting cock but it sure was better than being brutally tortured. Richie squatted down next to Dominick, placed his hand behind Dominick's neck, and squeezed it gently.

"Yeah man, you're a real good fucking sport..." Richie said to Dominick and tousled his sweat soaked hair.

"OHHHHHH man Richie, it feels fucking awesome, this guy suckin' my damned cock..." Bob gasped. "Fucking does it better than that bitch I'm seeing too. I'm goin' to pop my load already man..."

Richie stood up and ordered Dominick to keep Bob's cock in his mouth as he shot his load, making him swallow his juices. Dominick had never sucked a man's cock before, let alone swallowed his jazz, but at the moment he wasn't really in any position to argue against it.

"OHHHHRRRR man, yeah, swallow my load you fucking cocksucker..." Bob crooned as he came and came in Dominick's mouth. "OHHHHHHH shit yeaaahhhh man!!!"

When Bob was done he let his cock slip out of Dominick's mouth and Richie quickly took his place. Bob knelt down next to Dominick as the guy sucked Richie's cock and squeezed the back of my roommate's neck.

"Fucking best buddy I've ever known..." Bob whispered in Dominick's ear.

They made him suck their cocks twice each, each time making him swallow their juices. When they walked Dominick out of the bathroom a while later cum was caked all over his lips and his mouth was embarrassingly rancid with it. As they passed a clock in the hallway Dominick saw that it was nearing five PM. He wondered again how much longer it would all continue. As they walked down the stairs to the main floor of Richie's house Dominick looked down and took stock of his muscular battered body. His huge chest was striped from the beatings his two buddies had given it, his nipples were so very swollen and sore that he didn't even recognize them, his balls were still bound, swollen, and aching miserably, his cock looked all bruised and battered, the way no man's cock should ever look and the melted wax was still all over him. His ass cheeks and the backs of his thighs stung horribly and his muscular arms were totally fucking numb from having been roped up for so long at that point. Dominick realized that as the loser of the game he had to endure whatever else his two buddies might come up with. When they got to the bottom of the stairs Bob suggested to Richie that they should give Dominick a break for a while, adding that the guy was starting to look really beat. (Starting too???) Richie seemed to consider what Bob said, looking Dominick over.

"Yeah, maybe, maybe he could use some water," Richie said and he and Bob brought Dominick into the kitchen.

Bob sat Dominick in a chair and Richie poured ice water into a tall glass. Richie held the glass of water to Dominick's lips and my roommate sipped it down gratefully, whispering "thank you" to him in between sips. Bob stood behind Dominick, his hands resting on the big guy's shoulders.

"How much longer do you want to work him over for?" Bob asked Richie.

Richie glanced at the clock, smiled, and looked at Bob.

"A lot longer..." Richie said and he and Bob laughed meanly. "Drink up buddy boy, you need it..."

Dominick sipped the water down as Richie instructed, looking in his eyes above the rim of the glass.

"Starting to hate me eh buddy boy?" Richie asked Dominick. "I'll bet that when Monday morning rolls around and we're back at the construction job-site you won't even want to speak to me you'll hate me so much..."

Dominick finished drinking the water and Richie placed the empty glass in the sink. Standing by the sink he looked at Dominick with a smug expression on his face.

"I'll tell you Dominick, I've been planning this shit for a

long fucking time..." Richie said fiendishly. "Ever since you came on the job at Green and Sons I've had it in for you like this..."

"Wh-why??" Dominick asked him, needing to know.

"Because man, I watched you hauling those goddamned cinder blocks, those two by fours across your big shoulders, the coils of heavy duty wire under your big sinewy muscular arms... "Richie said, stepping over to Dominick as he spoke. "I watched you work in the hot sizzling sun with your shirt off, sweating your fucking guts out for all the guys to see, showing off for the women who passed by while we all worked. It all made me wonder just how much a guy like you could actually take if someone were dishing it out on him...I fucking wondered man..."

When Richie was standing over Dominick he grabbed a handful of Dominick's hair and yanked it hard, harder than earlier when he had grabbed the guy's hair in the same fashion.

"OWWWWWWWW!!!" Dominick cried.

"And now we're finding out aren't we Dominick?" Richie asked him snidely, pushing his head back and moving his face closer and closer to Dominick's as he spoke fiercely, sounding almost insane. "We sure as shit are finding out just how much crap you can take...we got you man, we got you so fucking good!! You're tied the fuck up, naked as the day you were born, fucking totally exhausted and beat to shit, and going nowhere anytime soon man. Shit Dominick, if I decide on it we'll keep you here overnight and work you hard all day tomorrow. And by now you know I can come up with a slew of shit to heap on you tomorrow."

As Richie spoke and yanked upwards on Dominick's hair Dominick's cock throbbed like crazy...in fear. He looked at Richie, his buddy, his fucking so called friend, with eyes filled with tears of terror. At that moment Dominick feared that his buddy had gone over the edge.

"Richie, please man..." Dominick croaked.

Richie let go of Dominick's hair and looked at him with that grin that Dominick had come to loathe.

"Bob lets get our buddy boy here up on the table," Richie said, hauling Dominick out of his chair and to his feet. "I just came up with a really painful idea..."

They hoisted Dominick up off the floor by his arms and onto the table on his stomach. Richie told Dominick to slide his knees under his stomach area. After the speech that Richie had just given Dominick didn't dare defy him. When his knees were tucked under him it caused his hard cock to stick out between the backs of his thighs, along with his bound, swollen and aching balls.

"What do you have in mind Richie?" Bob asked.

"You'll see, but man, he is going to hate it, that much I promise you..." Richie said, looking wildly at Dominick's cock and balls.

A few moments later Richie had tied a length of rope around Dominick's cock shaft and threw the slack of it over a beam in the low ceiling. He held the end of the rope in his hand and when he tugged on the rope it caused Dominick's hard cock to be pulled painfully up and held out straight and rigidly.

"OHHHHHRRR RICHIE, you bastard..." Dominick roared in agony. "Ohhhhh shit, my poor cock man!!!"

Slowly, Richie loosened his hold on the rope only to pull it up again, jarring Dominick's aching cock back up again.

"Ohhhhhrrrrrrr!!!" Dominick ranted, helpless on the table.

"Shit man, that is cruel Richie," Bob said with a grin on his face.

"Do you want to try it?" Richie asked Bob, offering him the rope.

"Sure as shit man," Bob said, quoting his buddy as he took the rope from Richie. "I'm just fucking glad that it's not me on that fucking table…"

With that Bob let Dominick's cock fall against the backs of his thighs but wasted no time tugging on the rope, getting Dominick's cock straight and rigid again. It was like being jacked off but in a horrible and really painful way.

"AYYYRRRRRR!!!" Dominick screamed as his cock suffered immense pain.

The rope tied around his cock shaft bit mercilessly into the soft and delicate skin there, causing the pain to feel thousands of times worse.

"Shit man, look at his cock twitch," Richie said as Bob tugged on the rope.

"Tell me man, if I had lost that fucking card game would you have done to me what you're doing to him?" Bob asked Richie as he let Dominick's cock down slowly.

"Would have had to man," Richie said, placing a hand on Bob's shoulder. "Rules of the game you know. But hey, we're all buddies here after all and we're just having some really intense and manly fun right?"

"Right..." Bob said and tugged on the rope again.

"R-right...AAARRRHHHHHH!!!" Dominick gasped loudly and his two buddies laughed.

Moments later Richie told Bob to tie the end of the rope he was holding off to the leg of the table that Dominick was laying on, keeping Dominick's cock straight out and painfully rigid.

"What do you have in mind now?" Bob asked Richie as he finished tying the rope around one of the table legs.

"Nothing he's going to like that's for sure..." Richie said and leaned down over Dominick's swollen and aching balls.

Bob quickly joined Richie in licking; squeezing, lapping and out-rightly torturing Dominick's already much wounded balls. He laid there roped up like a chicken with his poor cock tied and his tied balls being worked over...needlessly. Every time his two buddies closed their lips around his throbbing balls they got a good loud and piercing scream out of Dominick. He was crying again and praying (yes, praying) that it would be over soon. As they went on torturing his balls he felt one of them playing with the tip of his cock. Then, his manhood was being stroked. And then, Dominick shot the most painful and worst load of his life.

"OHHHHRRRR shit, you fuckers, milking me like a steer!!" Dominick gasped painfully as he squirted and squirted his juices. "Fucking perverts got me shooting my load again... AAARRRRHHHH man!!!"

They continued working Dominick's balls with their mouths a few minutes more and then Bob again came to my roommate's rescue, telling Richie that they had better stop because Dominick's balls were looking real bad…not to mention how awful his cock looked also. Richie listened to Bob's advice and untied the rope around Dominick's cock. Together, the two men got Dominick down off the table and stood him in the center of the kitchen. When Richie put away the rope they had used on Dominick Bob stood in front of my roommate, ran his hands through his sweat soaked hair, and again kissed him tenderly on the lips.

"We need to talk when this is over man…" Dominick whispered to Bob. "Even my gay roommate doesn't kiss me as much as you do… As a matter of fact my gay roommate doesn't kiss me. Fucker just slurps at my nips and licks my damned feet."

Bob smiled and kissed Dominick again. But then, Richie was back. He looked Dominick over, nodded his head, and said that Dominick was looking too relaxed, adding that it was time to put the screws to him again…the hard fucking way… Dominick rolled his eyes in disbelief. Richie opened a kitchen drawer and took out two long wooden spoons. He handed one to Bob.

"Remember when you were a kid Bob and your mom would threaten to beat you with a wooden spoon if you disobeyed her?" Richie chuckled, looking at Dominick menacingly. "Well, our good buddy here didn't disobey us but he is about to take a trip down memory lane…"

That said Richie gave one of Dominick's muscular upper arms a good hard whap with the bottom part of the wooden spoon that he was holding.

"OWWWWWW!!!" Dominick cried out and then Bob whapped his other arm really hard. "OWWWWWW!!!"

Standing at his sides they each whapped Dominick's

upper arms over and over, harder and harder with each blow.

"AAAAARRRRHHHHH shit..." Dominick gasped loudly. "Fucking bastards..."

When the arm that Richie was whapping was practically red all over he moved to Dominick's chest and whapped one of his poor aching and swollen nipples with his wooden spoon.

"OHHHHRRRR you fucker, my poor goddamned tits!!" Dominick roared in Richie's face and Richie quickly gave his other nipple another hard whap. "OWWWRRR!!"

Bob gave Dominick's upper arm a few more hard whaps with his wooden spoon and then began whapping Dominick's mid section, really hard, getting some real good hearty grunts of agony from him. As Richie beat on Dominick's nipples alternately Bob really seemed to delight in whapping his mid section. Dominick tried to tighten up his stomach muscles but by that point he was so fucking beat to shit and tired that it was nearly impossible. He clenched his teeth and did his very damnedest to endure the stinging burning pain of the wooden spoons. When Richie gave Dominick's ass the first whap with his wooden spoon Bob quickly followed his lead. Together they really whaled into Dominick's poor butt cheeks with those wooden spoons. They held him in place by his upper arms and bent him over slightly so that they could really get at his lower ass cheeks...and, according to Dominick if you've ever been whapped with a wooden spoon on your lower ass cheeks you know how horrible that pain is. With tears rolling profusely down his cheeks Dominick screamed and roared in a man's pain and tortured agony. He didn't beg them to stop because he knew they wouldn't...not until they had decided he had had enough. But how much was enough Dominick was wondering.

When they did stop beating Dominick's fleshy lower ass cheeks it felt as if they were literally on fire. Richie and Bob pulled Dominick to a straight standing position...his cock was sticking out long and hard (can you fucking believe that shit??) and his tied and aching balls were hanging down real low, begging for release from the rope that had been tied around them for hours now. Richie rubbed his wooden spoon over Dominick's hard cock and under it, hefting it with the spoon, a maniacal grin on his face.

"Oh man Richie, that really sucks," Bob said mockingly. "Are you really going to do what I think you're going to do?"

"Just one time Bob, real good and fucking hard..." Richie whispered as Dominick looked at him in pure terror, silently begging him not to, and his handsome face all scrunched up as his tears flowed and flowed.

But he did anyway; Richie raised his wooden spoon and gave the top section of Dominick's cock a good hard whap.

"Ayyyyyyyyyyyyyyrrrrrrrrr!!!!" Dominick screamed loudly and the room spun.

He fell to his knees, his head hanging down, his sweat soaked hair hanging in front of his face, and sobbed in agony, shaking and trembling like a little tree in a hurricane. Richie put the wooden spoons away as Bob stood over Dominick, a real look of pure concern on his face.

"Okay, now we're going to..." Richie began to say as he walked back over to Dominick and Bob.

"No man, that's it, he's had enough..." Bob said softly.

"What???" Richie asked him. "What do you mean he's

had enough?"

"I mean, he's had enough!!" Bob repeated, yelling now. "Look at him Richie!! Just look at the poor bastard!! He can't even breathe correctly he's in so much fucking pain!! We are not going to hurt him anymore man..."

Richie seemed to consider what Bob had just said and then Dominick's two buddies helped him to his feet. They untied his upper body and finally Richie untied Dominick's balls. Richie gave Dominick's balls a gentle tug and then my roommate's two buddies were standing at his sides. Dominick fell against Bob and he held him close as he sobbed and shook wildly, so glad that it was finally over...

"You're all right buddy boy," Richie said and squeezed one of Dominick's arms.

A short while later the three men were sitting in the living room. Richie and Bob were sitting on the couch and Dominick was sitting on a small love seat. They were all sipping cold beers. Dominick was dressed minus his socks and underpants.

"I know you probably hate me to some degree Dominick, but we're still buddies after all right?" Richie asked Dominick.

"Yeah, right..." Dominick said sarcastically. "Buddies..."

"I didn't mean it when I said that we would keep you here overnight and work you over all day tomorrow," Richie said. "I was just trying to scare you...you know, mind games and all that shit."

"Yeah..." Dominick said softly and looked at Bob, thanking God that he had made Richie stop the torture.

"Uh, is anybody hungry?" Richie asked. "I'm starving." "I'm a little hungry," Bob said. "What about you Dominick?" Dominick took a long chug of his beer and looked across the room at his two buddies.

"Yeah, maybe we could send out for a pizza or something," Dominick suggested.

He finished his beer, leaned his head back, and closed his eyes. He fell asleep almost instantly. He slept like that for a few hours and while Richie and Bob ate their pizza and drank another beer each. Dominick was so beat that he didn't even hear the doorbell when the pizza was delivered. Richie kept two slices of pizza for Dominick and warmed them up in the microwave oven when he woke up…at midnight.

"Holy shit, what time is it?" Dominick asked as he opened his eyes and stretched his aching body on the love seat.

"Midnight on the dot," Richie said.

Dominick ate his two slices of pizza, drank another beer, and chatted with his two buddies while they sat at the table in the kitchen.

"So, no hard feelings Dominick?" Richie asked him, holding out his hand for him to shake. "It was all in fun after all."

Dominick pretended to be angry for a moment, then, with a grin on his face he took Richie's hand in his and shook it.

"I'll give you a ride home if you want," Bob said to Dominick when he was finished with his pizza and beer. "I mean, you sure don't feel like walking right?"

"Yeah, thanks man…" Dominick said, knowing why Bob

wanted to drive him home.

Around twelve thirty they all said good-night, telling each other that they would all see each other on Monday morning at the job-site, and then Bob and Dominick left Richie's house. In the car Dominick slumped down in the passenger seat, ready to conk out again. He was so tired that it was unbelievable. Bob sat in the driver's seat and before he started the car he looked over at Dominick and placed a hand gently on his shoulder.

"You all right buddy?" he asked Dominick.

"Yeah, I guess so," Dominick said softly. "I mean, it's not everyday that a guy has his two best buddies in the world beat the living tar out of him you know."

Bob pulled Dominick close to himself and despite how bad he smelled he held the guy gently in his arms.

"Dominick…" he whispered and Dominick could feel Bob shaking.

"What's the matter man?" Dominick asked.

"Are you mad that I kissed you?" Bob asked him.

Dominick pulled away from him and started laughing.

"What's so funny?" Bob asked Dominick.

"Mad that you fucking kissed me man?" Dominick asked Bob, still laughing. "Bob, I was madder when you and that prick Richie were beating the tar out of me and torturing me…"

Bob smiled and started the car. Dominick leaned back in the passenger seat and relaxed.

"Dominick, I'm gay..." Bob suddenly said as he drove through the silent streets.

"Yeah, I uh, I figured that," Dominick replied. "And I kind of get the feeling that Richie is too."

"I think you're right," Bob said as he drove. "What about you Dominick?"

"I'm straight man, but I sure as shit have my fill of gay guys getting at me," Dominick replied, a sly grin on his face. "I mean, my gay roommate is wild for my nips and feet and you and Richie...well, you and Richie had at me in another way."

"I think a lot of times when guys are afraid to admit to their gay yearnings they'll use reasons like Richie's with the loser of the card game as excuses to get a guy naked..." Bob said, sounding very analytical. "...and once they have a guy naked they'll use torture and all kinds of erotic violence to express what they're really feeling. Does that make sense to you Dominick?"

"I suppose so..." Dominick replied and closed his eyes as Bob drove. "Now I think I know how my roommate feels when I make him lick my stinking feet at the end of the day... I fucking force it on him sometimes Bob, really make the poor fucker chow down on my smelly toes, suck the cheese out of them...and it feels so fucking good Bob."

When they got to the front of the apartment building Bob stopped the car and looked over at Dominick, his hand held out for him to shake.

"Friends?" he asked Dominick.

"Buddies..." Dominick said and pulled him close.

They hugged each other tightly and then Dominick stepped out of the car...

His story finished Dominick looked at me...

I was now sitting on the couch, across from where he was sitting. Actually, Dominick had not budged from where he was sitting since he had gotten home. He looked at me somberly, waiting for my comments.

"Your friend Richie sounds like a real sadistic bastard," I said an angry looking expression on my face. "I mean, what he did to your cock and balls are inexcusable man! Fucking stupid too...I mean what if he did permanent damage to you? And I have to say that as much as I respect Bob for coming out to you he was stupid for going along with it also."

"It was all part of the game Chris," Dominick said and ran a hand over his face. "But can I tell you a couple of things, just between us roommates man?"

"Sure," I said and Dominick gestured for me to go over to him.

I stood up, walked across the room, and squatted on the side of the living room chair that Dominick was sitting on.

"For whatever the fuck the reason I was so turned on by it all Chris..." Dominick said, looking at me intently. "But at the same time I was so fucking terrified. Does that make sense to you at all?"

"Sure it does," I said. "Sometimes what we fear the most is actually what turns us on more than anything. Sometimes we don't realize it until it's presented to us in some way...like what your two friends did to you today. It's kind of like a double edged sword."

Dominick seemed to think over what I had just said and then looked at me.

"There really was a strange yet erotic feeling going through me knowing that the two guys working me over were actually my two buddies…" Dominick said, rubbing the small amount of beard that had sprouted over his handsome face.
We looked at each other and I placed a hand gently over Dominick's crotch.

"You let your two buddies have at it, now how about letting your gay roommate have a go at it?" I asked him. "Let's make sure it still works…"

"Oh man, that's all I am to you eh, a sex object? Dominick asked me and we both laughed.

Dominick let me suck his cock but he told me to be real gentle about it. He was still aching there and on a lot of other parts of his body too…and would no doubt be hurting a few days afterward…

After I had sucked a good sized load out of Dominick he showered and went to bed. I waited about fifteen minutes to be sure he was asleep before making the phone call. When I heard the sounds of snoring coming from behind Dominick's door I picked up the phone and dialed. Richie answered on the second ring.

"Hello?" Richie said.

"It's me…" I said softly. "He's home…and he looks like

shit."

"Think we went too far?" Richie asked me.

"Not far enough asshole," I replied fiendishly. "Next time, and make sure there is a next time by setting up a card game real soon, next time don't be so goddamned soft with him. This fucking studly guy can take a lot more than we think."

Smiling wickedly I hung up the phone...

On Monday morning when Dominick arrived at the job-site where he, Richie and Bob were currently working they all agreed that it had been a great and interesting weekend. None of them brought up what had been done to Dominick...and haven't since.

After word from the author

I have always been fascinated by stories like the one you just read. It was an honor to write something so outlandish and over the top and in homage to a small novel that I happened upon years ago at this point. I would think that my fascination with stories like this one (both ones I have read and ones I have written) couples with and feeds my overwhelming lust for dominance and submission…

In "The Story of O" written by Pauline Reage a woman submits and allows herself to be used as a sex slave for a group of men. Because of her love for Rene she demands debasement and psychological tests.

In "That Day at the Quarry" written by Tom Shaw (the book that inspired "The Taming of Dominick") a young man agrees to the horrid consequences as the loser of a traditional game of poker. He becomes the property of the two winners and must allow them to do whatever they want with and to him for as long as they want anything short of maiming or murdering him that is.

In my story, "The Taming of Dominick", which echoes both of the ones I just mentioned a young handsome and muscular construction worker foolishly agrees to the terms of a card game put forth by his sadistic buddy. Dominick eagerly adheres to the horrid consequences of the game thinking there is no way he will lose. Inwardly, I believe Dominick's character mirrors me where my fascination with dominance and submission are concerned. After Dominick loses the game and is worked over for hours upon hours a revelation also comes for his buddy Bob so in a way I made this a "Coming Out" story as well...

Christopher Trevor

The Equipment
Dedicated To: Ray

I had just finished my daily workout and was in the kitchen sipping ice cold mineral water when the doorbell rang. I wondered who the hell it could be at 4:30 in the afternoon. I quickly put the water bottle in the refrigerator and grabbed my towel as I exited the kitchen. Shirtless, wearing just a pair of red cotton sweat soaked gym shorts and white sweat socks pushed down around my calves I walked to the front door. Glancing at the living room window as I padded to the door, wiping my muscular chest area of the sweat that was glistening all over it I saw the UPS truck parked outside my house.

"Alleluia!" I said happily, knowing what it was that was being delivered. "Sure took long enough for the stuff to get here..."

I had ordered the stuff a while ago so that when the doorbell rang that afternoon I had no idea who it could possibly be or why, until I saw the UPS truck parked out front. The doorbell rang again.

"Coming!" I called out.

I opened the door and standing there was a princely handsome UPS driver/delivery guy. He was just about as tall as I am; just a tad shy of six feet. He looked like a guy who worked out pretty regularly as well, just like me, seeing as his massive chest and pecs seemed to be straining in the confines of his short sleeved brown UPS uniform shirt. All this I took in very quickly as I glanced at him.

"Good afternoon, Mister Cordero?" he asked me; looking down at the electronic clipboard he was holding and then looking up at me in all my pumped up musculature.

For the briefest of seconds he seemed to drink in and devour the sight of my hugely muscular chest, my shoulders that are as wide as a doorway, and my size of bowling ball biceps.

"Yeah, that's me," I said, smiling a gentlemanly smile, me also taking in the sight of this dark haired, dark eyed handsome as a prince UPS guy.

We seemed to be sizing each other up, although for what, at that moment we still didn't know.

"Delivery Sir," he said to me in a very deep sounding voice, holding out the electronic clipboard and pen for me to take and then glancing down to the ground where two very large heavy-duty cardboard boxes had been placed.

"Wow, it came in two boxes eh?" I asked him, following his glance down to the ground where the boxes were.

I quickly took in the sight of the fact that he was wearing brown UPS uniform shorts, black work boots very highly shined and gleaming and those brown UPS socks with the two yellow stripes around the tops of them. Seeing as it was a hot August day it just made sense that he would be wearing uniform shorts rather than trousers. His legs looked like two tree trunks, thick and muscular; his calves were beautifully and massively defined just above his short socks.

"Yes it did Sir, and I have to say these two boxes are very heavy," he replied as I signed my name in the section marked for me. "Lugging them from my truck to your front steps was no easy chore."

"I'm sorry about that," I said kindly and handed him back his clipboard.

"Not a problem Sir goes with the territory," he responded and smiled his smile lighting up his entire face, nearly taking my breath away.

"Now, if you'll just lead the way and show me where you'd like the boxes placed I'll bring them in for you Sir," he said, put his clipboard down on top of the first box, turned his back to me, bent down to pick the heavy box up, bending his knees as he did so, making an exquisite outline of his cantaloupe shaped ass globes in his uniform shorts.

I held back a grunting gasp. I could tell from the way he was bent over and about to lift the first box that he was wearing trunk style boxer briefs under his shorts. They outlined magnificently under his uniform shorts. The muscles in the back of his legs were bulging and paramount as he bent to heft the box.
"Uh, that's not really necessary," I said as he amazingly hefted the box against himself, his massive chest heaving, his broad shoulders now pressing against his uniform shirt, beads of sweat forming on his huge neck and forehead.

"As I said Sir, not a problem, it goes with the territory," he said breathlessly. "Now, if you would lead the way…"

"Certainly, certainly," I said and pushed the door all the way open for him, holding it as he stepped inside with the first box. "Straight ahead through the living room to the smaller room just after it where I have my gym equipment."

"Yes Sir," he grunted and walked very wobbly and unbalanced toward the room I had indicated.

I watched from behind him as he lugged the box, the muscles in his big biceps straining beautifully, him suffering erotically. When he got into the room I had made into a workout area for myself he slowly lowered the box to the floor.

"Cool setup you got here Sir," he said to me, taking a cloth handkerchief from his pocket and mopping the sweat off his face, forehead and neck.

"Thank you," I replied.

"I'll go get the other box for you now Sir," he said and quickly walked past me back toward the front door, but not before stealing a glance at my big silver dollar sized fleshy nipples. (Or was I imagining that? I doubted it.)

As he walked past me I inhaled quietly and got a good whiff and nose full of his sweaty and over-worked aroma. This guy had been driving around and delivering heavy packages all I day I thought. I smiled as he bounced toward my front door, his cantaloupe shaped ass cheeks bobbing and swinging so fucking temptingly. I stayed right where I was in my workout room as he did the chore of getting the second equally as heavy box and lugged it just as he had the first one into my workout room. Sweating and gasping all over again he placed the second box right next to the first one.

"Thank you," I said to him as he straightened up and again with his handkerchief mopped the sweat off himself. "Can I maybe get you some cold mineral water?"

"That would be great Sir," he replied as he put his handkerchief back into his shorts pocket. "You're actually the first customer today to offer me a drink."

"Stay right here," I said to him and dashed out to the kitchen.

When I came back with a fresh bottle of cold mineral water a few moments later I found the princely handsome UPS guy looking over my weight bench and the rack of weights behind it. His eyes darted to my leg extension machine and the mat where I do stretching exercises and abdominal workouts. He took in the sight of my workout horse where I did gymnastic routines. I could tell that he was very impressed with my little gym area...

""This is some setup of equipment you have here Sir," he said to me as I entered the room, holding the bottle of water out to him. "Thanks for the water Sir. I truly appreciate it."

"You're very welcome," I said as he opened the cap and sipped down a long swallow of the icy cold liquid, me watching his sexy Adam's apple bob up and down as he drank. "Thank you for carrying those heavy boxes in here for me."

"You're very welcome, they're crates actually," he said and smiled that killer smile of his again. "It's not often that we have to deliver such big and heavy crates. May I ask what's in them?"

"Sure," I replied as I bent to start opening the first crate. "It's bondage equipment."

He had been about to take another sip of his water but when I said "bondage equipment" he stopped, holding the bottle just under his lips. I was guessing that he was expecting me to say that it was gym equipment in the box. I also thought that maybe he thought he'd heard me incorrectly...

"Bondage equipment?" he asked me and then sipped his water real fast.

"Yeah, it's for parties that I have from time to time," I explained as I savagely yanked the top off the first box.
"People that I know love to play around with shit like that. It's become a very mainstream type of fetish nowadays..."

"Bondage equipment," he repeated and stood nearly rooted to the spot as I pulled the packaging paper out of the first box. "Bondage equipment?"

"You've never seen stuff like this before?" I asked him, squatting down at the open box, reaching in it and producing a few lengths of average looking white cotton rope.

"Well, in magazines and things like that," he said, blushing slightly and trying not to appear all that naïve for his obviously twenty something years, I guessed twenty-two to twenty-three at the most. "I mean, I must have delivered shit, uh, stuff, stuff like that to other people, uh, other customers in the past but they never told me what was in the boxes, I never asked, I, I'm not supposed to, Sir... I mean, people, uh, customers can order whatever they want right? I'm not to question; I'm just supposed to deliver the shit, uh, the stuff, Sir..."

Realizing that he was babbling and blushing even more-so now he took another good gulp of his mineral water.

"What's your name?" I asked him, smiling reassuringly at him, still with the rope in my hand as I stood up straight.

"Jimmy Sir, Jimmy Mazza," he said.

"There's nothing to be embarrassed about Jimmy," I said

to him. "Lots of people use bondage equipment nowadays for a host of reasons, for fun, for competition, and even in the bedroom…"

"You know, that's just what I was telling my girlfriend just the other night and she thought I was crazy," Jimmy said and finished off his mineral water, looking a little more cooled down at that moment.

I planned to heat him up again though…

"Ah, so you have heard of stuff like this," I said.

"Well, yeah, sure," he replied, putting his empty mineral water bottle down on the box atop his clipboard. "I mean, I was just seeing if she would want to experiment you know? But like I said she thought I was crazy, asking me why I would want her to tie me up in bed, or anywhere else for that matter…"

So it was he who wanted to be tied up I thought happily…

"I see," I said softly. "Well, if you had more time and didn't have other deliveries to make I would have gladly given you a demonstration of some of this stuff Jimmy."

"I don't have any more deliveries today Sir," he quickly replied. "You're my last customer for the day."

"Ah, then perhaps I could show you the ropes so to speak, if you're really that interested," I said, stepping close to him and holding up the lengths of white rope temptingly in front of him.

His eyes were open wide in anticipation…

"Well, I've never used bondage equipment on anyone

before Sir, hell, I've never tied anyone up either," he said with a silly but adorable looking grin on his face.

"Ah, I see, then I suppose it makes sense that I'll use some of the equipment on you," I said as he reached forward and gave the rope I was holding a squeeze.

I could see that his hand was shaking and that his palm was slick with sweat...

"Uh yeah, I suppose that makes sense Sir," he said as he stroked the length of rope as I held it in front of him.

"What I teach you you'll be able to tell your girlfriend all about," I said softly as he let go of the rope and nervously licked his exquisite looking lips.

"Are you sure Sir?" he asked me. "I mean, I don't want to impose on you and all, I mean, you might have plans for this afternoon and..."

"Jimmy, step over to my workout horse and take off your uniform shirt and wristwatch," I said to him. "Lessons will begin now..."

"Okay Sir," he said and did as I said.

As the young handsome muscle boy stepped over to the workout horse I quickly dragged the first (opened) box closer to where he was. He unbuttoned his brown UPS shirt, the armpits areas of it were sweat stained as was the area that had been tucked down in his shorts. His chest and pecs were smooth, beautifully sculpted with muscles; Michael Angelo could have used this kid as a model. His biceps were big and round, curved and sinewy looking. His shoulders were broad and looked pumped, as if he had been lugging heavy boxes all day. His stomach was washboard and firm looking…

I had to hold back a gasp again as he bared his chest, draping his shirt over my weight rack followed by taking his wristwatch off and dropping it in the breast pocket of his shirt.
"What now Sir?" he asked me, standing and facing me practically at attention.

I looked at him and pretended that I was mulling something over.

"I think I'm forgetting something, but it's no big deal," I said with a smile and held up the lengths of rope. "Let's start off easy with this, rope…"

"Okay Sir," he said.

"Turn, lean over the workout horse and place your hands and wrists at the sides of the metal handle bars on top of it," I said instructionally.

He quickly did as he was told and I stepped in front of him to inspect how he had placed his hands and wrists on the metal bars of the horse.

"Curl your fingers and thumbs into fists, but not too tightly," I said to him and he did so. "First rule when tying someone up is that you don't want to cut off their blood circulation, got that?"

"Yes Sir, got that," Jimmy said, looking at me in anticipation.

"Okay, don't be scared now," I said and began looping the first length of rope around and around his right wrist, cinching it to the metal handle of the horse.

He looked down in awe, watching with his eyes wide open and his mouth dropped open a bit as I tied his wrist.

"Holy shit," he whispered as the rope caressed and snugly held his wrist.

"Are you alright?" I asked him.

"Yeah, I'm fine, great," he replied as I knotted the rope a few times, thus securing his wrist to the handle and insuring that he could not pull free either.

I quickly went to work on his tying his other wrist to the other handle...

"Shit," he whispered again and I could hear the mixture of fear and excitement in his voice as he watched me expertly loop the rope and knot it. "I-I'm being tied up here..."

"You certainly are Jimmy, you certainly are," I said and then moved a few steps away from him to look him over. "How does that feel?"

"I-I'm not sure," he said, tugging on the ropes. "I mean, lets face it, it feels confining but yet it feels awesome at the same time. Does that make sense?"

"Sure does," I replied and stepped over to my box of equipment that the guy had delivered, never once thinking that he would see the stuff used on its maiden voyage. "Now you'll have taken note I'm sure of how I looped those ropes around your wrists and then knotted them three times, that's the most you should knot ropes. You'll also note that I knotted the rope under the handles of the workout horse. Do you think you know why?"

"I-I'm not sure Sir," Jimmy said, looking down at his bound hands and tugging on the ropes.

"I knotted the rope under the handles so that there's no chance of you using your fingers to get to the knots, that way the only way you'll get free is when I untie you," I told him, stepping back over to him with the long metal ankle bar and leather thigh strap I had taken from the box. "Does that make sense to you?"

"I guess it does Sir," he said.

"If you tie someone up you don't want them to get untied until you untie them," I said, trying to sound sinister at that point, wanting to take this handsome prince on a ride to the land of fever. "Do you understand that?"

"Uh yeah, I do Sir," he said, watching as I placed the ankle bar against the horse and draped the thigh strap over it, right near his right sided bound wrist. "Uh, what are those?"

"This is an ankle bar and this is a thigh strap," I said to him, looking down at his feet. "Jimmy, I just remembered what it was that I forgot to ask you to do."

"What's that Sir?" he asked me and as he moved his legs slightly apart I was treated to the sight of the big chubbed up bulge in his uniform shorts.

"Well, in order for me to demonstrate the ankle bar and thigh strap I should have asked you to take off your boots and uniform shorts," I said to him. "I'll have to untie your wrists so that you can…"

"No, no, it's okay man, Sir," he said quickly, seeming to be reading my mind and wanting to reassure me at the same time.

"You can take 'em off me if you need to."

"Are you sure Jimmy?" I asked, already squatting behind him to get his boots unlaced.

"Sure man, Sir, I mean fuck it, I've been in locker rooms in less than my damned under shorts you know? We're just guys here after all..." he said, trying to sound sure of himself but obviously nervous at the same time. "And one time when a buddy of mine injured his arm lifting weights I had to help him out of his gym gear. So go ahead and get my shorts and boots off me, its okay...it is, really, its okay, Sir..."

"Okay then," I said happily and unlaced his right sided boot first, but slowly, very slowly.

"I just have to warn you though Sir," Jimmy chuckled as I began the task of slipping his first boot off him.

"What's that Jimmy?" I asked him, sounding unsure all of a sudden.

"Heh, my socks and feet stink after a long day encased in those boots," he said. "My girl friend, man, she can't take the stink. You got to hear how she bitches at me if I take my boots off just to relax when I'm at her house..."

"I think I'll be able to deal with it Jimmy," I responded reassuringly and then slowly slid his right boot off his foot, revealing his moist thin cotton brown trademark UPS sock.

He had balanced himself on his left foot as I lifted his right foot just below the calf and slid his boot off him... The guy was right. His socks and feet stunk. As soon as I had his boot off the scent emanating from it and his socked foot was overpowering. But as I said I was able to deal with it. Holding his boot in one hand and still holding his right foot by the calf and up off the floor with my other hand I slowly brought his boot up to my nose and mouth followed by hoisting his socked foot a tad higher off the floor.

"H-hey," Jimmy said, looking down and trying to stay balanced on his left foot. "What are you doing Sir?"

He watched in fascination as I held his boot over my nose and mouth and inhaled deeply while at the same time hefting his foot a bit more, my hand now holding tight to his socked ankle.

"Holy shit," Jimmy whispered. "Th-this isn't an easy balancing job Sir."

"Keep your tied up hands fisted and concentrate on your left foot Jimmy," I said to him as I placed his rank boot on the floor. "Don't worry what I'm doing with your right foot."

After placing his boot on the floor I bent his leg back a bit and then pressed my nose and mouth lovingly against the bottom of his right socked foot. His brown sock was moist and sweaty, his foot and arch beautifully imprinted against it, and his sock was literally matted to his sweaty foot. I placed his toes against my nose and inhaled deeply his musty and raw scent.

"Holy shit Sir," Jimmy said, looking down and watching with his eyes opened wide. "My girl won't go near my feet they smell so bad, and look at you sniffing them like they were the greatest smelling things on God's green earth."

"Maybe they are Jimmy," I replied and gently ran my tongue across his toes as he wriggled them in his sock.
I sniffed his arch and tongued it as well and then I planted what must have been more than a hundred gentle kisses on his heel, all over the bottom of his socked foot, the top of his foot and I

even kissed and sucked his toes for a good while…

When I was done I put his foot down on the floor and went to work unlacing his other highly shined boot.

"Damn man, Sir, you kissed my smelly foot," Jimmy said.

"And I'll do the same with this one as well Jimmy," I said as I slid his left sided boot off him, hefting that foot off the floor as he now stood balanced on his right foot. "I find that kissing a bondage novice's feet kind of puts them at ease…"

This time he faced forward and grunted and gasped as he felt my mouth, my tongue and my lips all over his other socked foot. After I placed his left foot back down on the floor I gripped both his ankles real tight. I loved handling his feet, they were so exquisitely shaped. Every part of him seemed a delight. The gods had really been smiling when they made him…

"Okay Jimmy, now I want you to hold tight to those handles that your wrists are bound to," I said to him, already starting to lift both his feet off the floor as I slowly stood up.

"Wh-what are you going to do Sir?" he asked me, sounding uneasy.

"Just want to stretch your legs out before I put the ankle bar on you," I explained and then in the next instant I had the guy stretched out in a prone (Superman flying) position.

"AHHHHHHH!!!" Jimmy groaned as I held his ankles and pulled hard, really stretching his muscular legs out, pressing the bottoms of both his socked feet against my nose and mouth again, kissing them, sniffing them heartily, drooling over his toes and sucking them into my mouth a few at a time. "AHHHRRRRRRRRR!!!!"

The kid held his tied hands in balled up fists and was in ecstasy as I stretched him and languished kisses and slurps all over his socked feet. He craned his neck as best he could to turn and watch me as I worked over his feet like crazy, pulling his legs and stretching them as much as possible. I kept at this for a good ten minutes and then finally set his feet back down on the floor.

"How do your legs feel Jimmy?" I asked him as I again squatted by the horse and began the task of getting his uniform shorts off him next.

"Uh, they feel wiry Sir, you really did a good job on 'em I guess," he replied. "Just can't believe that you sniffed and licked my socked feet."

I duly noted how this time he didn't make mention of the fact that I had also kissed his feet…

"It's a weakness of mine," I said, looking up at my prize with a sly looking grin on my face as I reached for his belt buckle. Looking down again the UPS guy watched as I undid the buckle of his belt and then reached even further to get at the button on his shorts. I pulled his zipper down and as I did I was able to feel the iron-like bulge he that he was sporting in his underwear.

"I'm glad you're enjoying all of this Jimmy," I chuckled as I slid his shorts down to his ankles.

"Sorry Sir, I have no control over my cock," Jimmy explained, blushing again. "Fucking thing is always hard and seems to have a mind of its own."

"I know just what you mean," I said agreeably, noting the rage hard-on in my own shorts. "I'm sure that your girlfriend appreciates that though."

"She sure does Sir," he stated proudly. "She sure as fuck does at that..."

His underpants were frosty white cotton, as I said earlier when I could see the imprint of them against his shorts they were trunk style boxer briefs, very sexy on him. I don't think this muscle headed kid had an ounce of fat on his beautifully sculpted muscular body...

I put his shorts aside and then looked up at him with a searching look in my eyes...

"Okay Jimmy, in order for me to properly demonstrate the thigh strap for you I'll need to have your underpants off you," I said to him, sounding unsure. "If you don't want that then we can skip the thigh strap and just get to the ankle bar."

"Take my underpants off?" he asked, pursed his lips and stifled a gulp.

"Yes, unless you don't want me to," I said and innocently placed a palm over one of his exquisitely cantaloupe shaped ass globes.

It was hard and smooth to the touch under his white boxer briefs and he took a deep breath.

"I will leave your uniform socks on you though," I said to him. "There'll be no need to take them off when I put the ankle bar on you."

"You're uh, you need to, um, God, you need to take my underpants off me but you're going to leave my socks on me huh?" he asked, sounding totally unsure.

Of course in his mind it made more sense for me to take his socks off him and leave his underpants on him, but that wasn't how it was to be for the handsome prince.

"Exactly Jimmy, unless you don't want me to, as I said," I began.

"No, no, it's okay man, Sir, like I said I've been naked in locker rooms," he said and I gave his butt cheek a fast squeeze before getting to the task of taking his boxer briefs off him.

After he consented I squatted behind him and gently gripped the sides of his underpants, ceremoniously and slowly pulling them down and off him, revealing two of the most succulent and delectable ass cheeks I had ever seen. MY GOD! As I said they were shaped like two cantaloupes and they looked as creamy as a bowl of fresh whipped cream. It was going to be my pleasure to redden them a bit once I had him fully the way I wanted him…

Still looking downward he watched as I placed his underpants in one of his boots, leaving them sticking out.

"Heh, interesting place to put my under shorts," he chuckled.

"Okay, now for the ankle bar Jimmy," I said and reached over and grabbed the metal adjustable device. "This is used in bondage scenes to keep the recipients legs stretched and well spread."

"Okay Sir," Jimmy said.

"Now if you want when I demonstrate this I can still take your socks off you, but as I said it's not totally necessary, so I'll leave it up to you," I went on.

"Uh, no, leave my socks on me, that's cool Sir," Jimmy replied.

"So with all that in mind I'll need you to please spread your legs as wide as possible," I told him.

He stifled a gulp but seeing as he had already gone this far I supposed he figured that he may as well do as he was being told. He licked his lips and then I watched as he parted his legs a little at a time, giving me an extraordinary view of his most private parts from behind. His hole was a rosebud, totally pink and moist looking in there, the scent emanating from it was raw and funky as I squatted close behind him. His juicy looking kiwi sized testicles dangled real sexy between his thighs, hanging down real low, no doubt chock full of his man juices. I gripped one of his socked ankles and forced him to spread his legs even wider than he was doing...

"Good boy Jimmy," I said and then encased first his right ankle in the bar.

I took note of the fact that his cock was beyond hard and pointing straight up under the workout horse he was tethered to. It twitched every few seconds and even dribbled droplets of pre cum. I had no doubt whatsoever that this kid was totally enthralled by all he was learning today...and I had only gotten started on him. After the ankle bar was locked onto his right ankle I adjusted the length of it and locked the other end around his left ankle.

"God, what a position this is," Jimmy commented, looking down and behind himself. "This really puts a person on display huh Sir?"

"Sure does," I replied in a very deep sounding voice and

gave one of his spread ass cheeks a hard friendly slap.

"OUCH!!" he said.

"Now for the thigh strap Jimmy," I said to him and reached up to take the leather device off the side of the horse.

"Yes Sir," the UPS prince said, wiggling his legs and trying to stay as balanced as possible with the ankle bar on his feet.

I adjusted my position behind him and squatted real close in at his thighs, my face not all that far away from his rosebud. His hole smelled real raw, sweaty and funky. I wrapped first the right side of the thigh strap around his right upper thigh and cinched it real tight before snaking it across his spread thighs and then securing his left thigh. In the center of the thigh strap is a long thin leather string, used to tie around the recipients testicles. Without asking his permission this time I gathered the kid's juicy balls in one hand, pulled them as far back under his ass crack as possible and slowly wound the thin leather string around them.

"HUHHHHH!!!!" Jimmy sighed real loudly as I handled his most private of regions. "I-I didn't think you were going to tie up my balls too Sir."

"Oh I'm going to do a lot of things to you that you had no idea about Jimmy boy," I teased him as I tied his balls at the base.

"God damn man," the kid whispered in passion and fear at the same time.

When I was done binding his balls I slowly moved them back so they would dangle again between his strapped thighs, but this time with the string holding them aloft… His cock was harder than it had been before I had tied his balls.

"And that my new buddy is how you would tie a person to a workout horse," I said as I stood up straight and next him. "What do you think?"

"Interesting," Jimmy said, looking down and taking in the sight of himself and then looking at me quizzically. "But if I were to say tie my girlfriend up like this I wouldn't have any use for that leather string on the thigh strap."

"No, that's only used for guys, obviously," I said to him agreeably.

"Okay, this is cool, totally cool," Jimmy said. "But once you have a person tied like this, what do you do to them next? "

"Well, that's a very good question Jimmy," I said, again sounding very sinister. "Because the answer is quite simply, that you can just about do anything you want to a person tied up the way you are now."

He then watched as I stepped over to the opened box that he had delivered and I took out a brand new round leather paddle.

"Along with the bondage equipment I ordered I also ordered some necessary accessories," I said to him, holding up the paddle.

"So I see," Jimmy said, sounding despondent now. "Oh holy shit…"

"I see you have the idea of what I meant about being able to do whatever you want to the tied up recipient," I said and rubbed the paddle over his delectable ass cheeks. "Were you in a college fraternity by any chance Jimmy?"

I gave his ass cheeks a hard whack with my leather paddle, the sound of it echoing through the room.

"OUCHHH!!" he seethed and looked up at me with his lips quivering. "Yeah, I was in a college fraternity Sir!"

"Did your pledge master paddle you?" I asked him and gave him another hard and resounding whack with the paddle.

"OUCHHH!! Yes Sir, he did, and then some, practically every night when I got back to my dorm room," Jimmy said.

"Then you know what you're in for now Jimmy," I said.

"I'm not sure I am Sir," he quickly explained. "You see, my pledge master used to use a wooden paddle on me that had holes in it. He never used a leather one like the one you have there."

"Not to worry Jimmy I have one of those as well and I promise to use that on you too," I said laughingly. "For now I want to use the leather one to warm your ass globes up a bit…"

"M-my ass globes, geez, no one ever called 'em that before," he said and I whacked his ass cheeks real hard again. "OUCCCHHHH FUCK!!!"

"Okay, I'm going to give you fifty swats with the leather paddle Jimmy," I said to him and he looked at me woefully, so much so that I almost felt sorry for him. "Now I'm not going to kid you here buddy, it's going to hurt. Five to ten swats with a leather paddle is enough to have a guys ass globes hurting. Fifty is going to have you burning and stinging."

"Y-yes Sir," Jimmy said and I could see he was holding back his tears.

"After your fifty swats I'll undo you from the horse and the ankle bar and the thigh strap," I explained to him, caressing his globes with the paddle. "After I undo you we'll move on to your next lesson where I'll bind you to my weight lifting bench. Got all that?"

"Yes Sir, I got it, got it all," he replied.

"Okay then lets begin, I want to hear you count each swat real loudly Jimmy," I instructed him. "If you miss a number or repeat a number by mistake I'll start back at the beginning. Think you can handle that too?"

"I'll do my best Sir," he responded, trying to sound as confident as possible.

"Begin!!" I barked and brought the leather paddle down hard on his glorious looking ass globes.

WHAPP

"One!!" Jimmy cried out.

WHAPPP WHAPPP WHAPPP

"T-two, three, four!! OUCHHHH!!!" he cried out louder. He balanced himself most precariously on the ankle bar and his tied balls swung beautifully between his thighs as he took the paddling.

WHAPPP WHAPPP WHAPPP WHAPPP

"F-five, OUCHHH, six, seven, and eight!!! OUCHHH!!!"

the kid blubbered as his ass cheeks started getting a nice sheen to them. "FUCK, I'm bein' spanked here!!!"

"You certainly are Jimmy, now concentrate," I said to him sternly and brought the paddle down again and again on his ass globes.

WHAPP WHAPP WHAPP WHAPP WHAPP

"Uh, n-nine, ten, OUCCHHHH, eleven, twelve, and thirteen, OUCCHHH!!!" he responded and counted dutifully.

Before continuing I rubbed his ass cheeks with the paddle for a few seconds, soothing him just a bit, but then...

WHAPP WHAPP WHAPP

"F-fourteen, fifteen, sixteen!!!" he called out loudly.

WHAPPP WHAPPP WHAPPP

"Seventeen, eighteen, nineteen, OUUUCCCHHHH!!!" he now sniveled.

Through the entire spanking the kid's erection didn't soften once.

When I got to the twenty fifth swat he was counting through clenched teeth, his eyes squeezed halfway shut, and he was sweating and doing his goddamned best not to cry.

"T-twenty five!!!" he called out pitifully at that point, his head hanging down, his ass globes red as a beet.

"Halfway there Jimmy, you're doing very well so far," I said in a complimentary manner.

"C-could we stop at twenty five Sir?" he asked me desperately. "I really do get the idea that you can do pretty much whatever you want to a person tied up like I am..."

"Now Jimmy, that is a ridiculous question," I replied and quickly brought the paddle down again on his delectable globes. "COUNT!!"

WHAPPP

"Twenty six!!! SHIT!!!" Jimmy seethed.

By the time I reached the fiftieth swat it must have seemed an eternity to the poor prince of a guy. His head was down and he had given in, he was crying. His ass cheeks were beyond beet red at that point. They were fire engine red...

When he called out the number fifty he sounded as if he had just scored a hard victory of some kind...

"Very good Jimmy, very well done," I said to him, gently caressing the back of his big neck as he stood there crying.

"Th-thank you Sir," he sniveled.

"Now I'm going to undo you from the horse but you are not, I repeat, you are NOT to rub your ass globes," I said to him. "Is that clear and understood?"

"Yes Sir, totally clear..." the UPS guy whimpered and I quickly untied his wrists from the handles of the horse.

As I squatted behind him to undo the thigh strap and the ankle bar he remained standing there crying and inspecting his wrists at the same time, taking in the fact that there were no rope burns on them whatsoever; the kid was impressed. He was hurting and stinging but he was also impressed...

When the thigh strap and ankle bar were off him I gave him a few minutes to stretch out his legs and thighs before getting to the task of binding him to my weight lifting bench...

"Feeling okay so far Jimmy?" I asked him as he stood on the rubber mat stretching, his ass globes well reddened and making a beautiful spectacle as he stretched.

"Except for my ass globes, as you call them I'm fine Sir," he replied.

"Another minute of stretching and then get over to my weight lifting bench," I said, stepping again over to my opened box of equipment and taking out this time a few leather straps.

"Yes Sir," Jimmy said and gulped hard when he saw the straps. "Holy shit..."

Moments later the UPS guy was standing beside me at my weight lifting bench. His cock was still rock hard and now pointing straight up at Heaven it seemed. I marveled at the thick droplets of pre cum that oozed from it every few seconds... Also, I want to point out how he looked so muscularly vulnerable somehow standing there in just his brown UPS socks, totally submissive to me and what I was teaching him. Teaching him? Fuck, I was having the best time of my life.

"Okay, now I'm going to show you the proper way to strap someone to either a bench, or a table or some other kind of apparatus," I said to him as he looked lustfully at my huge chest and then fearfully at the array of black straps I was holding. "Are you ready?"

"Y-yes Sir," he replied. "Ready..."

"Okay, on your back on the bench," I said to him. "Arms pressed hard at your sides and feet together. Got it?"

"Got it Sir," Jimmy replied and grimaced as his red ass cheeks made contact with the cushioned bench.

He quickly stretched himself out on his back, pulling his huge muscular arms against his sides and pressing his socked feet firmly together, just as I had instructed him... His chest made a real nice display as his nipples seemed to suddenly jut up and his cock pledged allegiance to me it seemed as it stuck straight up like a huge stalk between his well muscled thighs...

"Okay Jimmy, when strapping someone down there are two things that I like to keep in mind," I said to him, squatting down at his side as I spoke, taking in the glorious sight of his nipples and his huge pecs as he tried hard to stay stretched out and rigidly balanced on the thin bench.

Once he was strapped down those problems would go away...

"T-two things Sir?" he asked me.

"Yes, two things, the first of course is that when you strap a person down you're doing so because you want them immobilized, but yet not so tightly that they can't breathe," I said. "Secondly, the straps should be placed over the recipient so that you showcase the parts of them that you find to be most attractive."

"Showcase Sir?" he asked me. "That part I don't under-stand..."

"You will Jimmy, you will," I said and started strapping him down at his feet first.

I tethered the first strap just above his socks, allowing a little skin between his socks and the strap to show, I explained how I was showcasing that little patch of skin. I told him how lots of people find that little patch of visible skin to be very sexy and very erotic. He said that he understood and I pulled the strap tight, thus securing his ankles to the bench. Next, grunting, I strapped down his calves and then his thighs areas. With his head raised he watched in awe as I tethered him to the weight bench, his cock rigid and stalked up between his legs, his juicy, juicy balls resting atop his thighs…

I then secured a strap over and around his waist, directly under his cute and very deep belly button, showcasing his cum oozing erection…and securing his wrists and hands to the side of the bench as well. When I explained again how I was now showcasing a certain part of his anatomy, his erect cock he said he understood and again (breathlessly) apologized for it being so hard, adding how his cock just seemed to have a mind all it's own…

"It's quite alright Jimmy," I said to him and gave his hard cock a playful squeeze.

"OHHHHH GAWD," the UPS prince groaned at my touch and that sent his head back down onto the bench and he looked helplessly upwards at the ceiling. "FUCK, awesome experience I'm havin' here man, Sir…"

"Glad to hear that Jimmy boy, I'm very glad to hear that," I said to him and then secured a strap tightly around his upper torso, directly under his pecs and nipples, at the same time pinning his arms to the sides of the weight bench.

Lastly I placed a strap directly above his nipples so that the one under it and this one now showcased those great big nipples, those luscious tits of his to proportions that I bet he'd never imagined. Squatting beside him I pulled both the strap under his nipples and the one above his nipples a tad tighter than the other straps I had secured him with.

"AHHHHHHHHH!!!" he groaned and arched his head back a bit, all the while I was watching to make sure the kid was not in any intense pain.

The only pain he was actually in at that moment I think was the pain of desire and need, need because I think more than anything he wanted to shoot that pent-up load that was stock piling in his succulent balls. All this was indeed turning him on; there was no denying that...

"Feels okay Jimmy boy?" I asked him and ran a hand over his chest.

"Y-yeah, I suppose I am," he replied and was only able to raise his head now as he looked down at his strapped down self, his nipples jutted up and totally erect, sensitive looking actually and his cock totally stalked and twitching between his thighs, his balls churning. "Gawd, look at me here..."

Smiling, I leaned a bit more forward and balanced myself on my haunches. I then reached over him and gave each of his erect nipples a good hard squeeze followed by a mean twist.

"OOOOOOOOHHHHHH!!!" the kid groaned throatily and squirmed in ecstasy under the tight and binding straps. "FUCK, no wonder you "showcased" my damned man tits..."

"Man tits, I like that Jimmy," I said to him with a grin. "Actually I like it so much that I think those "man tits" of yours deserve another good squeeze and twist..."

124

And so, again I treated Jimmy's big sensitive nipples to a hard squeeze and followed up by twisting the fuck out of them…

"OOOOOOOOHHHHHH!!!" he groaned again, his head lay back on the bench as I let go of his "man tits." "FUCK, what an education I'm getting here huh Sir?"

"You could very well say that Jimmy," I replied as I got to my feet and towered over him, taking in the glorious sight of the handsome UPS muscle boy wearing just his brown uniform socks strapped down to my weight lifting bench.

"I have a question Sir, if I may," he panted, looking up at me hungrily in all my muscular glory.

"Sure thing Jimmy, ask away," I said and stepped down to the foot of the weight bench he was tethered to.

"Wh-when you have a person in a bondage position like before when you had me tied to the workout horse and now the way you have me strapped to this bench, how long should you keep the person that way?" he asked.

"Usually it's for as long as you would want to keep them that way," I said, squatting down at his sweaty and musty socked feet. "But if you tell them that you will release them at a certain point in time, its best that you keep to your word."

I placed a hand over his toes and gently caressed them. "If you don't release the person at the time you said you would you've breeched the trust that that person has put in you," I went on and then leaned down and pressed my lips against his smelly socked toes, inhaling deeply before continuing my answer to his question. "You always want to be able to have the person that you're going to restrain trust you Jimmy. Do you understand?"

"Yes Sir, I do, I truly do," he replied in a gasp, his head raised again and watching as I licked the bottoms of his socked feet.

"It would be the same way as you trusting me right now Jimmy," I said.

"Yes Sir, I do trust you," he said. "Fucking best delivery stop I made today..."

"Now I have a question for you Jimmy," I said with a grin and pressed my fingers of both hands against the bottoms of one of his feet each.

"Wh-what's that Sir?" Jimmy asked in reply.

"Are your feet ticklish?" I asked him and before he could utter a reply I began twirling my fingertips maddeningly against the bottoms of his socked feet.

"OHHHRRRRR Y-yes, ha, ha, ha, ha, ha, ha, ha, ha, ha, ha, ha, ha, ha, ha!!!!" he laughingly responded. "Oh yes, ha, ha, ha, ha, ha, ha, ha, ha, ha, ha, ha!!!! M-my feet are very f-fucking, ha, ha, ha, ha, ha, ha, ha, ha, ha, ticklish!!!! Ha, ha, ha, ha, ha, ha, ha, ha!!!!"

As I tickled the bottom of his left foot with the fingers of one hand I tickled the arch of his right foot with the fingers of my other hand...

"OHHHRRRRR ha, ha, ha, ha, ha, ha, ha, ha, ha, ha, ha, ha, ha, ha, ha!!!!" the poor kid laughed and laughed, bucking wildly under the straps, his head raised, his face turning red as he laughed harder and harder, his cock twitching like mad between his thighs, beads of piss along with pre cum now oozing from his wide sexy slit. "OOOHHHH, ha, ha, ha, ha, ha, ha, ha, ha, ha, ha, ha, ha, ha, ha, ha, ha, ha!!!! Pl-please stop Sir, ohhhhrrrr, ha, ha, ha, ha, ha, ha, ha!!!! Please stop t-tickling my feet!!!"

Instead I pressed my thumbs hard right into the balls of his feet and twirled them against his socks and from the way he then bucked on the bench I could tell that I was sending shock-waves through his very being…

"HA, HA, HA, HA, HA, HA, HA, HA, HA, HA, HA, HA, HA!!!!!!" he laughed louder now and cackled, his massive chest heaving and hawing under the binding straps, his "man tits" seeming to swell up on his chest, bigger than erect at that point. "Ha, ha, ha, ha, ha, ha, ha, ha, ha, ha, ha, ha, ha, ha, ha, ha, ha, ha!!!!"

"Remember something else right now Jimmy, commit it to memory because I'm only going to tell you all of this one time," I said to him sternly, still tickle torturing his feet.

"I-I'm listening, ha, ha, ha, ha, ha, ha, ha, ha, ha, ha, ha, ha, ha, ha!!!!" he squealed crazily. "I'm listening Sir!!!!"

"When you have a person restrained, anything you choose to do to them must be carried through to completion but at the same time it must be something that they are able to endure," I said to him. "Just as I paddled you earlier and am tickling you now. Do you understand what I just told you Jimmy boy?"

"I-I, ha, ha, ha, ha, ha, ha, ha, ha, ha, ha, ha, ha!!! I-I understand Sir!!!" Jimmy screamed as I went on and on and on tickling his feet.

I stopped tickling Jimmy's feet about twenty minutes later and then quickly undid the straps holding him to the bench. As I released him from under the straps he was still chuckling a bit, even though I was no longer tickling his feet. I wondered if he would bolt from my house at that point but he simply asked if he could please have some water before I got to the next event, as he so aptly called it, citing the fact that all that laughing and sweating through being tied and spanked earlier had made him real thirsty. Before dashing to the kitchen to get him a fresh bottle of ice cold mineral water I tied a black cloth blindfold over the studly kid's eyes, explaining how I didn't want him looking in the opened box of "bondage equipment" while I was gone. I didn't bind his hands behind him after blindfolding him, I simply told him that I had enough faith and trust in him at this point that he would not take the blindfold off. He smiled thinly and said "Yes Sir," as I guided him by one arm to a chair and sat him down in it...

Jimmy sat in the chair sipping his second bottle of mineral water a few minutes later, still blindfolded as I worked at setting up the next device from the opened box that he had delivered. I didn't want him seeing the device until I had the entire thing fully erected and set up. His cock was still erect and oozing pre cum as he sat there sipping his water while blindfolded. He looked so exquisitely vulnerable that it nearly stole my heart as I looked at him from time to time. He listened as I got the parts for the next device out of the box and set them up very quickly and efficiently. I was going to have to send a thank you note to the bondage company that I had ordered the stuff from. It was all perfect and all very easy to put together, just as they had said in their advertisement. And fate had sent the correct UPS guy to deliver it all to me. Looking at Jimmy again as he sat there blindfolded, totally submissive and obedient to me I thanked the gods and fate for bringing him to me, if only it would be just for that day, he did reference a girlfriend after all...

I had the next device that I planned to restrain Jimmy to set up less than twenty minutes later. Finished with his water now he stood beside me, still blindfolded, a look of anticipation etched on his handsome face.

"Okay, are you ready to see what you're in for next?" I asked him, my fingers on the knot in his blindfold.

"Ready if you are Sir," he said to me and his erect cock twitched at me.

I whipped the blindfold off him and as his eyes adjusted back to the light he took in the sight of the wooden "X" shaped structure I had mounted against a bare wall in the room we were in, in bondage terms the device is called a "Saint Andrew's Cross." As I said it is in the shape of an "X" and it also has leather restraints attached to each corner of it, restraints for the wrists and ankles.

"Holy shit," Jimmy said and took a few steps forward, really drinking in the sight of the cross now, touching the leather restraints on it. "I can only imagine how much all of this shit, sorry Sir, all of this stuff cost…"

"It's okay Jimmy," I said, stepping behind him and giving the back of his beautiful bull-like neck a gentle squeeze. "Are you now ready to take your place?"

He looked at me, looked at the cross, looked at me again, gulped hard and said, "Yes Sir…"

I positioned him with his ripped muscular back against the cross and instructed him to stretch his arms and legs out against the sides of the device in an "X" shape before I got to the task of binding him to the structure… I first locked his wrists into the leather restraints, tight, but as always, not tight enough that he wouldn't be able to squirm in them. The way his arms were pulled upwards now gave a wonderful view of his peach fuzzed armpits and it also outlined his shapely triceps muscles superbly. With a curious look in his eyes he watched as I sniffed his randy deep armpits after having gotten his wrists locked in the restraints.

"I'm not going to lie to you Jimmy or try to sugarcoat it for you, what I have planned for you while you're mounted on this cross is going to be intense," I said to him, a menacing look in my eyes as I said it.

Jimmy's eyes opened wide in sudden fear, no doubt he was thinking how I had been trustworthy up till this moment and now I intended to do him real harm. And being that his wrists were already locked against the cross there was nothing he could do to stop me. Instead of comforting him and putting his mind at ease I simply squatted down at his feet that I had come to be so enamored and in awe of and next secured them in the leather restraints at the bottom of the Saint Andrew's Cross.

"Sir, please," Jimmy whispered as I then wound a strap around his chest, lashing that part of his body securely to the cross.

He squirmed perfectly and just as I wanted him to within the restraints on his wrists and ankles, dancing a sort of sexy dance for me at the same time…

"Sir, please," Jimmy said again and when he repeated it a third time I almost felt sorry for him.

"Remember what I told you Jimmy boy," I said to him, squeezing his nipples as I spoke softly but sternly. "When you have a person restrained they have to be able to deal with what-ever torments and tribulations you plan to heap on them. It's a matter of them trusting you. And you as their tormentor have to know that they can deal with it…"

He looked at me beseechingly and with tears in his beautiful eyes; I twirled and whirled his nipples, his man tits, his succulent and hard man tits, I held the tips of them and twisted and twirled them… The kid grunted and gasped as I played his nipples like an instrument… He moaned and groaned somewhat contentedly and lustfully at the same time…

"I know that you'll be able to handle what I'm about to do to you Jimmy," I said to him, softer yet, still holding tight to his nipples, squeezing the fuck out of them. "I wouldn't be about to do it if I didn't think that you could handle it…"

That said I let go of his nipples and stepped back over to the open box of bondage equipment… Jimmy's eyes opened wider and his tears nearly flowed from them when he saw the thin riding crop I took from the box…

"Just as you counted the swats I administered to your ass globes earlier, you're to count off the lashes that I'm about to dispense to your chest and armpits Jimmy," I said, rubbing the tip of the riding crop seductively and teasingly against one of his very jutted up and beyond sensitive at that point nipples, his "man tits."

He simply stared at me in outright horror, knowing that I would not release him from the cross, knowing that he had to see this through…

"Heave that chest forward for me Jimmy boy, this time we're going for a total of one hundred lashes, chest and armpits combined," I said to him.

He looked at me, clenched his teeth and then did something that made me proud, he nodded his head up and down, silently telling me that he was ready…

I turned away from him for a moment so that he wouldn't see me smile with the pride I felt for him at that moment…

Then, I took up position a few feet away from him and raised my riding crop…

"Chest first and then armpits Jimmy boy," I said sternly and he instantly pushed his mighty chest out above the strap that was wound tightly under it.

WHACK

"One!!" Jimmy called out and I quickly whacked his chest a second and third time in fast succession. "Two, three, OUCCHHHHHH!!!"

WHACK WHACK WHACK WHACK went my riding crop against his chest and then against his left armpit quickly followed by the right sided armpit.

"f-four, five, six, OUCCCHHHH!!!! S-seven," the kid railed angrily, with total and sheer determination showing in his eyes.

By the time I reached the thirtieth whack Jimmy's chest was red with stripes and sexy looking and his armpits were sweating, stinking and also stinging pretty badly I had no doubt. He was crying, sputtering, miserable and trying to count all at the same time…

WHACK WHACK WHACK WHACK

"th-thirty one, thirty two, OUUCCCCCCHHHH, OHHHRRRRRR GOD, please Sir, please!!! Thirty, thirty three, thirty four!!!" he screamed and ranted at me.

He didn't know it but if he miscounted on this particular event or lost count there was no way that I would make him start the count again back at the number one. I simply wanted him to endure what was being done to him, I wanted him to enjoy being mounted on the cross and of course to feel proud of himself when it was over, but sadly the UPS prince still had a way to go…

WHACK WHACK WHACK WHACK

"th-thirty five, thirty six and thirty seven," Jimmy sputtered through his tears of anger. "And thirty sev, no, thirty fucking eight, FUCK!!!! OUCCCHHHHHH!!!!"

A few times my riding crop connected meanly with the tips of Jimmy's nipples, really getting the kid screaming and squirming on his cross prison. When I was finally done whacking him one hundred times with the riding crop the UPS guy was a sniveling, shaking and trembling mess. But he had done it, he had endured it well. When he had screamed out the number one hundred I got the feeling that he must have thought he'd died and gone to heaven. I put the riding crop back in the box and stepped over to the cross to release him… As I undid the restraints on his feet and then on his wrists I wondered if this was it, if he would tell me to go fuck myself, get himself dressed and storm the fuck out of my house. Instead, what he did shocked me totally… When the restraints were off his wrists he stepped forward, nearly falling forward actually off the cross and threw himself into my big muscular arms. I held him tightly against me as he shook, sweated and trembled, but he had stopped crying. He held tight to my shoulders, his face buried against my neck as I held him tighter against me. After a short while more of this he got himself composed and under control and then asked me what the next device was that he would be tied up to… At the sound of those words I held him tighter still, our hard cocks rubbing against each other, his totally exposed and mine in my gym shorts…

I wasted no time in getting my UPS prince into the next demonstration of some of the equipment that he had delivered to me and was now experiencing firsthand. Before getting to the task of restraining him again I ordered Jimmy to go stand in front of my rack of weights that was behind my weight benching bench, with his back to the weights.

He quickly did as he was told, his hard cock leading the way as he stepped over to the weight bench. While Jimmy stood waiting for what I would do to him next I took from the box the next pieces of bondage equipment that he would get to experience… He was about to experience irons… When he heard the rattle and noise of the iron items that I took from the large box he simply stood by the weight rack, not once turning around to see what I was up to…

Moments later Jimmy's hands were locked behind him in an old fashioned pair of handcuffs with a thin metal chain looped to the center of them. The other end of the thin metal chain was wound and fastened to the weight bar behind where his cuffed hands were. As I had begun the task of binding my bondage student in the irons I made sure to tell him that he must remain rigidly still throughout the entire event. Iron restraints do not stretch if one happens to squirm and pull on them while locked in them. Jimmy said "Yes Sir" and stood still as I stood at his side and locked his upper arms in a metal bar with lock-up shackles on the sides. The iron arm bar was heavy and the kid now needed to use the strength of his biceps to keep himself standing in the position I had now had him. Squatting in front of him I put an iron thigh strap on him next. It was the same fashion as the leather thigh strap I had put on him earlier when I'd tied him to the workout horse, except that there was no attachment with which to tie his balls up with. Lastly I put a pair of shackles with a chain attached to them onto Jimmy's socked ankles, fastening the chain to the weight bar behind him at his feet. Looking down at himself Jimmy took in the sight of himself in metal restraints and his cock stiffened still more, if that were possible...

"How does that feel?" I asked him.

"Heavy Sir," he replied and jutted his chest forward, the irons on his arms obviously uncomfortable for him.

"You'll get used to it," I said to him and stepped back over to my opened box of equipment. "Now remember well what I told you about not moving around when locked in metal restraints Jimmy."

"I'll remember Sir," Jimmy called out as I rummaged in the box behind him until I found what I was looking for.
Smiling wickedly I stepped back in front of my prize holding up a pair of sharp teethed nipple clamps, or in Jimmy's case, "man tit" clamps.

"I'm glad you remember Jimmy boy, because this is going to have those sore "man tits" of yours screaming and it's going to make you want to squirm like a fish out of water," I said and before he could even react I clipped the clamps tightly onto the meat of his big fleshy nubs.

"OHHHHH SHIIITTTTT!!!" Jimmy squealed as the tit clamps chewed meanly at his poor nipples. "OWWWWRRRR GAWD Sir!!!"

The kid moved only his head back and forth, his teeth clenched tight; his eyes scrunched up and nearly shut tight...

"N-no wonder you beat on my "man tits" earlier with that damned crop," he seethed as I held the chain between the clamps and tugged on it a bit, really stretching his "man tits" for all they were worth. "Y-you wanted my "man tits" really sore for this shit, OHHHRRRR Sir!!!"

His cock twitched and his balls swung and churned direct- ly over the metal thigh strap as the kid did his best to endure what I was doing to his nipples. I let the chain go for a few sec- onds and then gripped it again, tugged on it till his nipples were meanly stretched again and this time held it that way...

"AYYYRRRRRR!!!!" the UPS guy seethed and looked down at his shackled feet. "D-don't move, w-won't move..."

"Atta boy Jimmy," I said to him encouragingly. "If you move you could wind up hurting yourself real badly."

Then, I let go of the chain between the clamps and quickly grabbed the little knobs on the sides of them that controlled the pressure of them. If the kid thought that the clamps were tight right now on his nubs he was in for a big surprise. He watched, looking down as I twisted the small knobs and suddenly the sharp teeth of the clamps were bighting harder and harder on his "man tits."

"OWWWWCCHHHHH!!!!" Jimmy reeled, his head thrown back, looking up at the ceiling miserably.

I tightened the clamps to fullest capacity and then let go of them...

"HUHHHHHHH   HUHHHHHH!!!!   OHHHHRRR FUCCKKK!!!!" Jimmy panted, looking down again, looking down directly at his nipples as they suffered in the clamps.

He balled his cuffed hands into two fists behind him and squealed mightily as I took the chain of the clamps in hand again and tugged at it. With the immense pressure on his nipples and having the clamps tugged and his nipples stretched again the kid was obviously feeling a tad more than erotic pain... Sweat broke out beautifully all over his muscular chest and he swore and ranted like a captured marine as I worked and tortured his nubs erotically...

"Now Jimmy, there is something else I need to tell you through this," I said to him and loosened the tit clamps slowly. "Are you listening to me?"

"Y-yes Sir, I'm listening, I always listen Sir," he said, his voice filled with some relief as I loosened the clamps some more.

"If you lock someone in irons someday down the road, and I get the feeling that you will," I began, grinning. "And if like I've done to you, you choose to work them over with tit clamps you must only leave the clamps on their nipples for a maximum of no more than fifteen minutes. Do you understand that?"

"Y-yes Sir, I understand Sir," Jimmy bellowed.

"More than fifteen minutes can really damage a person's nipples Jimmy boy," I said and tugged again on the chain on his nubs, sending stinging and erotic pain through his very being. "When working a person's nipples with clamps the idea is simply to get them sore and sensitive, not to severely damage them."

"I- I got it Sir, I understand Sir!!" he cried and then I gently took the clamps off him.

"AYYYYRRRR SHIIITTT!!!" he screamed, balling his cuffed hands in and out of fists madly. "It, it feels worse now that you've taken those fuckers off me..."

"That's just the blood rushing back through your "man tits"

Jimmy," I said, explaining the sensation he was now feeling. "It passes quickly..."

"Glad to know that Sir!" the kid seethed as I began taking the metal restraints off him.

Within the scope of a few minutes Jimmy was free of the metal restraints and then found himself being tied by me into a leather strait jacket. He stood facing forward with his arms in the sleeves of the leather device, those arms yanked around him in opposite directions and pinned to his sides as I stood behind him wrapping him up very speedily. Admittedly this was one of my favorite devices to use; I'm expert with strait jackets...

"How does this feel Jimmy?" I asked the UPS guy as I pulled the straps on the strait jacket real tight around and around his upper body, pinning him into the thing.

"Like all the other things so far Sir, it feels very confining," Jimmy said. "It reminds me of those old fashioned movies where characters were committed to the nut house..."

We both laughed good naturedly at his comment...

"Well, during this event in your bondage experience I don't want you to be frightened Jimmy," I said to him.

"Oh, not to worry Sir, like I told you, I trust you completely," he said to me and my heart nearly melted.

"You're not understanding what I mean Jimmy," I said and from the box of equipment I produced a leather hood, complete with eye and mouth coverings. "Once I put this on you, you won't be able to see, or speak for a while. I want you to trust me completely Jimmy. I want you to totally give yourself over to me this time..."

"Gee, it matches the strait jacket," he said with a silly looking grin as I held up the leather hood.

His hard cock twitched and jerked a bit...

"Are you ready Jimmy?" I asked him and brought the leather hood close to his face.

"Sure, why the hell not?" he replied with a question of his own. "Ready, sure as shit, ready, sweating in my socks but ready nonetheless..."

I stepped behind him and slowly slid the hood over his head...

When it was over his head I snapped the eye coverings shut first, he inhaled deeply, the sound of fear mixed with excitement in his deep intake of breath. I then asked the kid if he had anything else to say before I gagged him...

He gulped hard and said, "No Sir," and I slowly slid the three inch dildo shaped gag into his mouth, filling his craw with it, before snapping it onto the leather hood.

"MMMMfffff..." Jimmy sputtered behind the gag and squirmed on his socked feet, his upper body squirming in the confines of the leather strait jacket.

From the opened box of equipment I got a bottle of lubricant, not just any lubricant mind you but a lubricant that when rubbed against flesh would warm up erotically...

I took my prize by his upper arm and led him over to the workout horse...

"We're going to end this in the same place where it began Jimmy boy," I said to him.

"Mmmmmff?" he asked me, walking awkwardly on his socked feet.

I placed him over the workout horse in a bent over position; his socked feet slightly dangling off the floor.

"Okay Jimmy, this time I'm not going to hurt you, I assure of you that," I said to him and squeezed a good dollop of the lubricant into my open palmed hand.

He nodded his hooded head up and down enthusiastically...

Then, with my lubricated palm I reached between his thighs and under the workout horse, gripping his hard as steel cock and yanking it forward under his ass crack...

"HHHRRRMMMFFF???" the hunky UPS guy grunted and his head shot up, nodding back and forth as I slowly began stroking his huge stalk. "MMMFFFFFFFFFF!!!!!"

His trapped arms thrust around in the strait jacket and he lifted his socked feet further off the floor, bending himself a bit more over the workout horse, an indication to me that he was thoroughly enjoying what I was now doing to him...

"RRRMMMFFFF!!!" he garbled and chewed and sucked on the dildo shaped gag filling his mouth.

I stroked him a tad faster and then I could feel the lubricant warming up a bit...

The kid's head snapped back when he felt the heat and I

stroked his crank harder, watching as massive sized droplets of pre cum oozed from his wide sexy slit. His nuts were no doubt churning, getting ready to release their pent-up stockpile of the kid's juices.

"RRRMMMMhhhmmffff…" he snarled and bucked wildly atop the workout horse, his socked feet swinging at my sides, the scent emanating from them musty and erotic all at the same time.

He was obviously in a state of high ecstasy as I slowly jacked him off, slowly bringing him toward a gusher he obviously had never experienced before…

"Thinking about your pretty girlfriend Jimmy boy?" I asked him teasingly.

"MMMMMFFFF MMFFFFFFF!!!!" he sputtered, nodding his head no, then yes, then no, then yes again.

His cock warmed up some more as I stroked the lube against it, tightening my grip on it, thrusting it faster in my hand… His rosebud asshole twitched and winked at me as he spread his legs while I thrust his cock against his very visible ass crack. Then, the kid raised his head, looked upward with his covered eyes and roared, "RRRRMMMMFFFFF!!!" with wild abandon. His head fell forward and I could tell that he was gnawing wildly on the gag when his mess of creamy good stuff erupted from him…

"MMMMFFFFFFFF UUUMMMMNNNNFFFFF!!!" Jimmy grunted and gasped as his mess shot from him in torrents, filling my hand, slipping and sliding through my fingers like sand. "RRRMMMFFFFF RMMMFFFFFFF!!!!"

He swung his hooded head from side to side, his mess

seeming to erupt more and more from him rather than dissipating as I milked and milked and milked him...

When he was done I let go of his cock and he screamed out one final "RRRRMMMMFFFF' before I began releasing him, starting first with the hood, taking the gag out of his mouth.

"OHHHHRRRRR fucker, fucker, Sir," Jimmy panted breathlessly, his lips trembling as I slid the hood off him, his hair slightly mussed and sweated. "Thank you man, thank you, oh fucking fuck, thank you Sir!!!"

When I released him from the strait jacket he turned around and with tears in his eyes threw himself wildly into my arms... I held him tight as he cried tears of joy, saying "thank you, thank you, thank you" over and over. I softly whispered "you're welcome Jimmy" in his ear.

I had taught him well that day...

A while later I watched from my window as Jimmy the UPS driver walked back out to his truck, back in his uniform of course, well, not completely. As he drove away I held tightly to his socks that were in my right hand...

I smiled and a tear trickled down the side of my face as I watched the truck pull away...

Ten Years Later

I had just finished my daily workout when the doorbell rang. I wondered who the hell it could be ringing my doorbell at 4:30 in the afternoon. Sipping cold mineral water and dressed just in blue workout shorts and navy blue sweat socks tucked down around my calves I walked in all my muscular glory to the front door. The doorbell rang again…

"Coming!!" I called out and saw the UPS truck parked out in front of my house.

I smiled from ear to ear. The stuff was here. It was finally here…

I opened the door and standing there was a princely handsome and studly young blond UPS driver, the same way as Mr. Cordero had thought of me ten years earlier. On the ground at his feet were two heavy crates with my name and address on them…

"Mr. Mazza?" the UPS guy asked me. "Mr. Jimmy Mazza?"

I nodded "yes" as he held out his electronic clipboard to me, me smiling wickedly at the handsome young UPS guy…

ABOUT THE AUTHOR

Christopher Trevor was born in July 1963 and grew up in New York City. As soon as he was old enough to know how he began writing fiction and has been writing gay erotic/fetish stories for the past ten to twelve years at this point. He became an avid reader as well from the time he knew how and reads everything from fiction, to non-fiction to biographies of interesting and unusual people, people who have made a difference or who have paved the way for others. Christopher attributes his writing artistic inspiration to artists such as Etienne, Tom of Finland, Tagame, The Hun, and most notably Joe T, who Christopher has had the pleasure of speaking with and even meeting over the last few years. Christopher states, "Joe T encouraged me to write about my fetish because I was embarrassed about it at the time. Joe T said that when we are embarrassed about something that makes it even more enticing somehow." Christopher totally agreed and never stopped writing in this genre. Erotic writers who inspired Christopher Trevor were: Tom Shaw (author of "That Day at the Quarry), C.S. White (author of Big Sur), Larry Townsend (author of countless erotic novels), and Mason Powell (author of the classic story "The Brig.")

Christopher discovered that not only did he enjoy writing erotic tales but that after his first bondage experience he had a genuine flair for it. Writing to erotic oriented magazines about his first bondage experience truly opened the floodgates for Christopher where this style of writing is concerned. Christopher thanks the handsome and muscular "Greg" for that experience way back in time. Christopher took "Creative Writing" courses every semester during his high school years and while other friends of his stopped writing what they loved to write about as time went on Christopher never let a day go by when he didn't write something… "I feel that if I don't write every day I will die," Christopher has said many times over.

Foot fetish stories and all things related; spanking fetish, erotic shaving, muscle bondage, tickle torture, and hardcore stories are just a few of the areas of gay eroticism that Christopher enjoys writing about and inspiring in others as well. As one internet buddy said to Christopher where the black socks fetish is concerned, "Until I started talking with you I never gave a thought to my socks when I got dressed for work in the morning. Now when I pull my dress socks on every morning I get a chill up my spine."

Christopher is proud of the erotic effect he has on people…

Christopher Trevor is also the author of:

> The Executive Guide to Foot Fetishism and Office Discipline
> 1-887895-36-1

> Executive Ties That Bind
> 1-887895-37-X

> Don't!! Stop!! That Tickles!!
> 1-887895-31-0

Look for them where you found this book or Amazon.com.